The Party Fairies

To Ellie Delamere who loves fairies

Special thanks to
Narinder Dhami

ORCHARD BOOKS
338 Euston Road, London NW1 3BH
Orchard Books Australia
Level 17/207 Kent Street, Sydney, NSW 2000
First published in 2005 by Orchard Books
© 2007 Rainbow Magic Limited
Rainbow Magic is a registered trademark
Illustrations © Georgie Ripper 2005
The right of Georgie Ripper to be identified as the illustrator
of this work has been asserted by her in accordance
with the Copyright, Designs and Patents Act, 1988.
A CIP catalogue record for this book is available
from the British Library.
ISBN 978 1 84362 820 0
1 3 5 7 9 10 8 6 4 2
Printed and bound in China
Orchard Books is a division of Hachette Children's Books,
an Hachette Livre UK company.
www.orchardbooks.co.uk

Grace the Glitter Fairy

by Daisy Meadows

illustrated by Georgie Ripper

ORCHARD BOOKS

www.rainbowmagic.co.uk

A Very Special Party Invitation

Our gracious King and gentle Queen
Are loved by fairies all.
One thousand years have they ruled well,
Through troubles great and small.

In honour of their glorious reign
A party has been planned,
To celebrate their jubilee
Throughout all Fairyland.

The party is a royal surprise,
We hope they'll be delighted.
So shine your wand and press your dress...
For you have been invited!

RSVP: HRH THE FAIRY GODMOTHER

Contents

A Party Afoot

"Isn't it a beautiful day?" Kirsty Tate said happily, looking up at the deep blue sky. "I'm so glad you're staying here for a whole week, Rachel."

Kirsty was sitting on the grass in the Tates' back garden, making a daisy chain with her best friend, Rachel Walker. Pearl, Kirsty's black and white kitten,

was snoozing in a patch of sunshine in the middle of the path.

"You know, Rachel," Kirsty went on, picking another daisy. "This is the perfect day for—"

"A party!" Rachel broke in, knowing exactly what Kirsty was going to say.

Kirsty nodded, a frown on her face. "Let's hope horrid Jack Frost's goblins don't spoil someone's special day."

"The Party Fairies will do their best to stop them," Rachel replied in a determined voice. "And so will we."

Rachel and Kirsty had a wonderful secret which no one else in the whole human world knew about. They were best friends with the fairies! So far, the girls had helped the Rainbow Fairies and the Weather Fairies against Jack Frost's evil spells. Now it was the turn of the Party Fairies.

"Isn't it just like mean old Jack Frost to want to spoil everyone's fun?" said Kirsty. "He can't stop causing trouble, even though he's been banished to his ice castle."

"If he hadn't been such a pest, he could have come to the surprise party for the Fairy King and Queen's 1000th jubilee," Rachel pointed out.

The girls had been invited to the
Fairyland party themselves, and they
had been very excited about it — until
they found out that Jack Frost was
determined to have a party of his own.
His goblins were causing trouble at
human parties, so that the Party Fairies
would appear to put things right. Then
the goblins would try to steal the fairies'
magic party bags for Jack Frost to use
at his party.

"Well, we managed to keep Cherry
the Cake Fairy and Melodie
the Music Fairy's party
bags safe," Kirsty said,
adding another daisy
to her chain. "We'll
just have to keep
our eyes open."

"And our ears," added Rachel.

Suddenly, there was a scrabbling noise behind the hedge. "OW!" someone muttered. "That hurt."

"Who was that?" gasped Rachel. "Do you think it was a goblin?"

Kirsty grinned and shook her head. "It's OK," she said. "It sounds like Mr Cooper, our next-door neighbour."

At that moment, Mr Cooper popped his head over the hedge. He was a tall, thin man with a cheerful smile. "Sorry, Kirsty," he said, "did I startle you?

I pricked my finger on the rosebush."
He held up a small parcel wrapped in
shiny blue paper. "I'm trying to hide
these presents around the garden for the
treasure hunt this afternoon."

"Treasure hunt?" repeated Rachel,
looking puzzled.

Mr Cooper nodded. "Yes, it's my son
Jamie's birthday today," he replied.
"He's five and we're having a party."

A party! Rachel and
Kirsty glanced
at each other
in excitement.

"We've got ten
children coming,"
Mr Cooper went on.
"And we've hired a clown called
Mr Chuckles. Jamie is really excited."
He smiled and shook his head.
"It's going to be a lot of hard
work, though."

Rachel nudged Kirsty, who knew
exactly what her friend was thinking.

"Maybe Rachel and I could come
over and give you and Mrs Cooper
a hand?" Kirsty suggested.

"Yes, we'd love to," Rachel
added eagerly.

Mr Cooper's face lit up. "That's very kind of you," he beamed. "Jamie would love that. The guests are arriving at three o'clock, so could you come at two?"

"Of course we will," Rachel and Kirsty said together.

Mr Cooper gave them a grateful smile, and went off to hide some more parcels.

Kirsty turned to Rachel, her eyes wide with excitement. "Do you think a goblin will turn up and try to spoil Jamie's party?" she asked.

"I don't know," Rachel replied. "But if one does, we'll be ready for him!"

Decorating Difficulties

"This is going to be fun," Kirsty grinned, as she rang the Coopers' doorbell. "Jamie is really sweet. It'll be a bit noisy, though, with him and all his friends running around enjoying themselves."

"Maybe they'll frighten the goblins away!" Rachel said with a laugh.

The front door opened. A small boy with exactly the same cheerful smile as Mr Cooper stood in the hallway.

"Hello, Kirsty," Jamie called eagerly. "Are you and your friend here to help with my party?"

"Yes, we are," Kirsty replied, smiling and handing Jamie a parcel. "Happy birthday."

Jamie tore off the wrapping paper excitedly and beamed when he saw the bright red car inside. "Thank you! Come on," he said, taking Kirsty's hand. "Me and Mummy are putting up decorations in the lounge."

Rachel and Kirsty followed him down the hallway. Mrs Cooper was standing on a chair, pinning a HAPPY BIRTHDAY banner to the wall.

"Hello, Kirsty," she smiled. "And it's Rachel, isn't it? It's so kind of you to help out. Thank you."

"Mum!" Jamie was dancing around the lounge, waving his new car. "Look what Kirsty and Rachel gave me! And can we put up the streamers now? Can we?"

"There's still an hour to go and he's already fizzing with excitement," Mrs Cooper said, laughing. "Would you girls be able to put up the streamers and balloons, please, while I go and help Jamie's dad finish off the food?" She pointed to a folded, gold-coloured paper tablecloth, and some bowls and plates which were on the table. "And if you have time, could you lay the table, too?"

"Of course we can," Rachel replied.

Mrs Cooper thanked the girls and hurried off to the kitchen.

Jamie grabbed the box of decorations from the sofa. "Daddy bought some new extra-long streamers," said Jamie proudly. "They're gold and silver – look!"

He began unrolling one of the streamers. But before he had got very far, a piece about fifty centimetres long dropped off and floated to the ground.

"Oh!" Jamie gasped.

"I'm sure the rest of it is OK," Rachel said quickly.

"Keep going, Jamie."

But as Jamie unrolled the streamer, more lengths of brightly-coloured paper fell off. Rachel opened the other packets, but those streamers had been spoiled in exactly the same way.

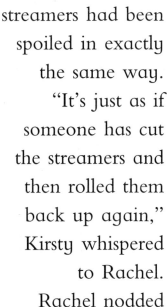

"It's just as if someone has cut the streamers and then rolled them back up again," Kirsty whispered to Rachel.

Rachel nodded solemnly. "Do you think it could be goblin mischief?" she asked.

Jamie was looking close to tears.

"They're too short!" he wailed.

"Don't worry, Jamie," Kirsty said, giving him a hug. "I've got just the thing to fix this. I won't be long."

Kirsty ran home and found a big roll of sparkly, blue sticky-tape, which was left over from Christmas. Then she went back to the Coopers' house and showed it to Jamie. "Look," she said, beginning to stick the pieces of one of the streamers together. "Now you'll have stripy gold, silver *and* blue streamers."

Jamie's face lit up. "They look even better now!" he declared happily.

The three of them quickly stuck the rest
of the streamers together and then Rachel
and Kirsty began to pin them up around
the room. They had just finished when
there was a ring at the doorbell.

"That'll be Mr Chuckles," Mrs
Cooper called from the kitchen. "Could
you let him in, please, Kirsty?"

"I think Jamie has beaten me to it,"
Kirsty chuckled, as Jamie dashed past
her into the hall.

Rachel and Kirsty followed him, and found the clown standing on the doorstep, smiling down at Jamie. He wore a bright blue, baggy suit and a blue bowler hat.

"You must be the birthday boy," he said.

"Where's your big red nose and your big clown shoes, Mr Chuckles?" Jamie wanted to know. Rachel and Kirsty smiled.

"Ah, well, I'm not quite ready yet," Mr Chuckles explained. "It's difficult to drive my van in big clown shoes."

Looking as if he was about to burst with excitement, Jamie ran to tell his mum about the clown.

Meanwhile, Mr Chuckles turned to Rachel and Kirsty. "Is it OK if I set up my stuff in the lounge?" he asked.

Kirsty nodded. "Yes, we've almost finished decorating," she replied. "We've just got the balloons to blow up."

The clown opened the back of his van

and began to unload his props, while the girls went back into the lounge. But to their dismay, the streamers which they had so carefully pinned up earlier had all fallen down. Now they lay in heaps on the floor.

"This has to be the work of one of Jack Frost's goblins!" Rachel said crossly, grabbing a streamer. "He must be here somewhere."

"Quick, let's get these back up or
Jamie will be upset," Kirsty said, picking
up the sticky-tape.

The girls worked fast and got the
streamers back in place before Jamie
came bouncing into the room.

"We're going to blow up the balloons now, Jamie," said Kirsty, opening one of the packets. "Which colour shall we start with?"

"Gold!" Jamie called eagerly.

Kirsty began to blow air into the long gold balloon. But although she huffed and puffed and got red in the face, the balloon wouldn't inflate. It remained as flat as a pancake.

"There's a hole in it," Rachel said, peering closely at the balloon.

The girls exchanged a look. They were both thinking exactly the same thing.

"The goblin again!" Kirsty whispered. Quickly, she and Rachel checked all the other balloons. There were holes in all of them! Jamie's bottom lip was trembling. "Are all the balloons spoiled?" he asked in a small voice.

At that moment, Mr Chuckles came into the lounge carrying a large wooden box. "Is it balloons you need?" he asked. "I've got some spares." He put his hand into his pocket and pulled out a handful of different-coloured balloons. "I use them to make my balloon animals."

Kirsty and Rachel were very relieved to see Jamie smiling again. Quickly, they blew up the balloons and hung them around the French windows at the far end of the room.

Suddenly, the doorbell rang. Jamie peeped out of the front window. "It's Matthew, my best friend!" he shouted excitedly. "And Katie and Andy and Ben. It's time for my party to start!" And he dashed out to meet his guests.

"Goodness me, I must go to the bathroom and put my clown make-up on," said Mr Chuckles. He grabbed a small case and left the room.

POP! POP! POP!

Kirsty and Rachel jumped and turned round. The balloons they had just put up were bursting, one by one.

"I'm starting to get very fed up with that goblin," Rachel said crossly.

"So am I," Kirsty agreed. "We need to find him and put a stop to his tricks!"

The doorbell was ringing again as more guests arrived, and the girls could hear them chattering excitedly in the hall. They didn't have much time to find and stop the goblin.

Then they heard Mr Cooper's voice. "Follow me out to the garden, kids," he was saying. "We're going to have a treasure hunt!"

There was a loud cheer as the children hurried after him, and Rachel and Kirsty looked at each other in relief.

"Let's search the room," Kirsty suggested. "We might be able to deal with the goblin while everyone's in the garden."

But just as they began their search, Rachel groaned with dismay and clutched Kirsty's arm.

"What is it?" Kirsty whispered.

"Look!" Rachel said, pointing towards the French windows. "Outside in the garden."

Kirsty peered through the glass to see a sparkling pink shape flying swiftly through the air. It was zooming straight through the garden, towards the French windows of the lounge.

"Oh!" Kirsty gasped. "It's Grace the Glitter Fairy!"

"Yes," said Rachel anxiously. "And the children are going out into the garden. They'll all see her unless we do something – and fast!"

Saving Grace

"We have to go outside and warn
her," Kirsty said.

"What about the goblin?" Rachel
asked.

"This is more important," Kirsty
replied, opening the French windows. She
and Rachel rushed outside, waving their
arms madly to get Grace's attention.

Grace saw them straightaway and
waved her sparkling pink wand at
them. She had long, straight, glossy
blonde hair, and she wore a glittering
rose-coloured dress, which shimmered in
the sunshine. The hem of the dress was
red and cut into handkerchief points.
The floaty skirt swirled around her legs
as she hovered in mid-air.

"Hello, girls," she called, "It's good to see you—"

"Grace, you have to hide!" Kirsty burst out, without even saying hello. "The party guests are about to come out into the garden any minute!"

Before Grace could say anything, they heard the back door open.

"So that's what you have to do, kids," Mr Cooper was saying. "Off you go."

Grace looked alarmed as all the children came galloping out of the back door. "Thanks for warning me, girls," she gasped. And she fluttered out of sight behind a garden urn filled with flowers.

The children were running all round the garden now, screaming with excitement. Two little girls came over to where Kirsty and Rachel were standing, and began to search for presents there.

"Er, I think Mr Cooper hid most of the presents down the bottom of the garden," Rachel said quickly. She didn't want the little girls poking around and finding Grace.

One of the girls ran off straight away,
but the other one frowned.
"I can see something
sparkly behind
that pot," she said
stubbornly, pointing
at the urn. "It might
be one of the presents."

"Oh, no," Kirsty said, thinking fast.
She bent down and picked Grace up,
keeping the fairy out
of sight in her hand.
Then she popped
her in her pocket.
"That's just
an empty
sweetie wrapper."

"We'll put it in the
bin with the rubbish," Rachel added.

The girl looked disappointed and ran off after her friend. Kirsty and Rachel sighed with relief.

"Rubbish?" Grace said, poking her head out of Kirsty's pocket. She looked a bit flustered and her hair was all messy. "That's nice!"

"Sorry, Grace," Kirsty said soothingly. "We didn't mean it."

"There's a goblin here," Rachel told Grace, as the little fairy smoothed down her hair. "He's been ruining all the party decorations in the lounge."

"Well, we'll soon put a stop to that!" Grace declared, looking outraged.

"Where is he?"

"We don't know," Kirsty replied. "We were just about to start looking for him, when we saw you coming."

Grace nodded. "Well, now I can help you find him," she said, smiling. "Lead the way!"

As Kirsty led the way through the French windows into the lounge, she suddenly gasped and caught Rachel's arm. "Look, there!" she breathed. "Behind the curtain."

Rachel and Grace looked at the long blue curtains hanging either side of the French windows, and immediately saw what Kirsty had spotted – behind one of them, there was a definite goblin-shape!

An Uninvited Guest

They all stared at the goblin bulge behind the curtain. They saw it shift once or twice. The goblin was obviously getting a bit fed up.

Kirsty beckoned Rachel and Grace to follow her to the other end of the room. "We need to do something right now," Kirsty whispered.

"Before Jamie and his friends come in from the garden."

"Yes, but what?" Grace queried, biting her lip anxiously.

The three friends racked their brains to think of a plan.

"We could creep up on the goblin and grab him while he's wrapped in the curtain," Rachel suggested. "It shouldn't be too difficult. He's quite small." Rachel knew that Jack Frost's magic could make the goblins much bigger and scarier when they were in the human world, but as the Fairy King and Queen had taken Jack Frost's magic away for one year, the goblins were their normal size.

"Then Grace can quickly magic him away to Fairyland," Rachel added.

Grace nodded enthusiastically, but Kirsty looked worried. "He'll try to fight his way out," she said. "What if he ruins the curtain?"

"Well, it's made of really thick material," Rachel pointed out. "I don't think the goblin will be able to do much damage."

"And I can fix it with Fairy magic once I'm back in Fairyland," put in Grace. "And then I'll whiz back here and magic it into place for you, too."

"OK, let's give it a try," Kirsty agreed.

She and Rachel crept cautiously
towards the French windows, with
Grace fluttering alongside. They had
nearly reached the goblin, when the
lounge door suddenly opened and
Mrs Cooper appeared, laden with
plates of food.

Quick as a flash,
Grace darted
into Kirsty's
pocket, out
of sight.

"Ah, girls,"
said Jamie's mum.
"Could you possibly
give me a hand with these snacks?"

Rachel and Kirsty exchanged an
agonised look, but there was nothing
they could do.

"Yes, of course," Kirsty replied
politely, and the girls hurried to help
Mrs Cooper set the plates down on the
dining table.

"As soon as the children have finished
the treasure hunt, we'll bring them
in here," Mrs Cooper told the girls.

"They can have a snack before they watch Mr Chuckles, and then after his show, we'll have tea."

The girls nodded and Mrs Cooper headed back to the kitchen.

As soon as she had gone, Grace fluttered out of Kirsty's pocket and the girls turned back to tackle the goblin. But it was too late!

"Oh, no!" gasped Rachel, as she looked around the room. All the streamers lay on the floor again. The decorations were ruined. But, worse than that, the goblin-shape behind the curtain had vanished!

"Well, at least I can set these decorations to rights," Grace said, reaching into her pocket for her party bag.

But Kirsty stopped her. "No, you mustn't," she said in a low voice. "That's exactly what the goblin wants you to do. He's hiding somewhere – just waiting for the chance to snatch your party bag!"

Goblin Trap!

At that very moment, the three friends heard a scrabbling noise behind the sofa!

"The goblin must be hiding over there," Rachel whispered excitedly, pointing to the sofa. "And he's heard us talking about the party bag."

Kirsty's face lit up. "That's it!" she whispered. "We'll use Grace's party bag as bait to catch the goblin."

"I know how we can grab him, too,"
Rachel added quietly. She pointed
at the paper tablecloth,
which Mrs Cooper
had bought for
the party. "We'll
wrap him up
in the tablecloth
instead of the
curtain, and then Grace
can still whisk him off to Fairyland!"

"Good idea," Grace whispered.
"We'll hide behind that armchair, and
catch him red-handed." Then she spoke
again in a louder voice. "My party
bag's so heavy, girls," she said with a
wink. "It's because I've got so much
magic fairy dust in it."

"Why don't you put it down on the coffee table?" Rachel suggested, glancing at the sofa.

"Then you can come into the kitchen with us, and we'll show you Jamie's beautiful birthday cake," added Kirsty, picking up the shiny, gold-coloured tablecloth. "It's in the shape of a steam train."

"OK," Grace agreed. She pulled her sparkly blue party bag from her pocket, and placed it carefully on the coffee table. "Let's go then."

But instead of leaving the room, they all tiptoed over to the armchair, and hid behind it. It was a bit of a squash. Kirsty and Rachel were too big to both fit behind the chair.

"Rachel, your feet are sticking out," Grace whispered. "Wait a moment."

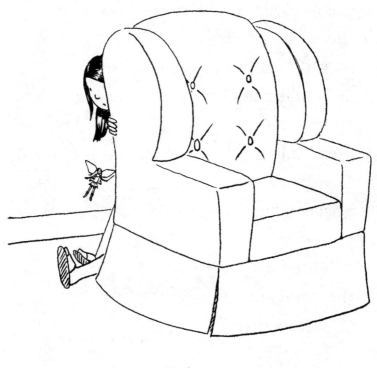

She twirled her blue wand in the air and there was a sparkle of fairy dust. In a second, Rachel and Kirsty had shrunk to fairy-size, with glittering wings on their backs. As tiny fairies, it was easy for all three friends to fit behind the armchair. Kirsty fluttered her wings happily.

Grace looked pleased. "That's better," she said, glancing at the sofa. "And we're just in time. Here he comes..."

The goblin poked his head round the
edge of the sofa to see if the coast
was clear. Then he
stepped out, a big
grin on his mean
face. His beady
little eyes gleamed
as he saw the
party bag lying on
the coffee table,
and he hurried to pick
it up. "Jack Frost will be
really pleased with me," the goblin
chortled smugly.

But as he reached for the party bag,
Grace, Kirsty and Rachel zoomed out
of their hiding place, each holding a
corner of the tablecloth.

"Get him!" Rachel yelled.

They hovered above the surprised goblin, and dropped the tablecloth right over him. He gave a shout of fury as it covered him completely from head to toe.

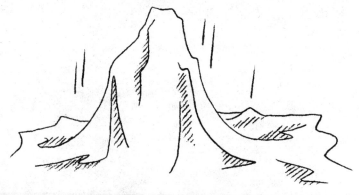

"It worked!" cried Kirsty.

"Now, let's wrap him up more tightly," Grace said.

But before they do so, the goblin began to rip the tablecloth to shreds!

All Wrapped Up!

"He's tearing his way out!" Kirsty
exclaimed. "What shall we do?"

Rachel looked round, spotted the streamers
on the floor and had an idea. She grabbed
the end of one of them, and flew swiftly
round and round the goblin, tying him up.

"Quick, Kirsty!" Grace called, as she saw
what Rachel was doing. "Grab a streamer."

"Stop it!" the goblin called crossly. He tried to fight his way out, but Grace and the girls were wrapping him up too quickly. A few minutes later he couldn't move. He looked just like an Egyptian mummy.

"Ohhh!" the goblin groaned sulkily.

"Serves you right," Rachel told him, as Grace rescued her precious party bag.

Meanwhile, Kirsty had fluttered over to the French windows to check on the treasure hunt.

"OK, kids, you've found all the presents," Mr Cooper was saying. "Now it's time to see Mr Chuckles, the clown."

"Jamie and his friends are coming in now, Grace," Kirsty called. "You'd better go."

Grace turned to the goblin. "And you're coming with me," she laughed. She waved her wand, and the moaning, grumbling goblin disappeared in a cloud of sparkling fairy dust.

"Goodbye, girls, and thank you,"
Grace said. She gave
them a hug, and
with a wave of her
wand, made them
human-sized again.

Then Kirsty
remembered the decorations.
"Grace, can you help?" she asked,
pointing at the streamers and balloons.

Grace nodded and smiled. She tipped up
her party bag, and emptied all the fairy
dust into the lounge. Tiny, shining
diamonds whirled and swirled around the
room, spinning into every corner.

When the magic dust had cleared, Kirsty
and Rachel were delighted to see that the
walls were festooned with glittering,
rainbow-coloured streamers and balloons.

There was even a new, gold, paper tablecloth, and when Kirsty and Rachel spread it out on the table, they saw that it was shinier than before and covered with a sprinkling of gleaming silver stars.

"Thank you!" the girls cried in amazement.

Grace gave a silvery laugh, waved her wand and disappeared, just as the children charged in led by Mr Cooper. They all stopped and stared in amazement at the fabulous decorations.

"Wow!" Jamie gasped. "Look what Kirsty and Rachel have done, Dad!"

"It's fantastic, girls," said Mr Cooper gratefully.

Rachel and Kirsty beamed at each other, and sat down with the party guests to watch Mr Chuckles perform. The clown was very funny and had everyone in fits of laughter with a giant, water-squirting sunflower. Rachel and Kirsty enjoyed it just as much as Jamie and his friends.

At the end of the show, Mr Chuckles told them he was going to make some balloon animals. When he opened his bag and pulled out a handful of balloons, there was a gasp of wonder. They were the most wonderful, colourful balloons anyone had ever seen – and some were even striped and spotted with animal-print designs.

Mr Chuckles stared at them in delight. "I didn't even know I had these," he muttered.

Rachel and Kirsty smiled. They knew where those balloons had come from – Grace the Glitter Fairy!

Mr Chuckles began to twist and tie the balloons together. He made an elephant first, which he gave to Jamie. Then he made a lovely giraffe and a zebra.

"These are for the two girls who put up these beautiful decorations," Mr Chuckles said. He bowed, and presented the giraffe to Rachel and the zebra to Kirsty. The girls were thrilled.

And so was somebody else…

"This is my best birthday ever!" Jamie beamed, as the clown began to make animals for all the other children.

"And we've saved another Party Fairy and her party bag," Rachel whispered happily to Kirsty. "Hurray!"

The Weather Fairies

Thanks to real fairies
everywhere

Special thanks to
Sue Bentley

ORCHARD BOOKS
338 Euston Road, London NW1 3BH
Orchard Books Australia
Level 17/207 Kent Street, Sydney, NSW 2000
A Paperback Original

First published in 2004 by Orchard Books.

© 2008 Rainbow Magic Limited.
A HIT Entertainment company. Rainbow Magic
is a trademark of Rainbow Magic Limited.
Reg. U.S. Pat. & Tm. Off. And other countries.

HiT entertainment

Illustrations © Georgie Ripper 2004

A CIP catalogue record for this book is available
from the British Library.

ISBN 978 1 84362 636 7

24

Printed and bound in China by Imago

Orchard Books is a division of Hachette Children's Books,
an Hachette Livre UK company

www.hachettelivre.co.uk

Evie
the Mist
Fairy

by Daisy Meadows
illustrated by Georgie Ripper

ORCHARD BOOKS

Goblins green and goblins small,
I cast this spell to make you tall.
As high as the palace you shall grow.
My icy magic makes it so.

Then steal Doodle's magic feathers,
Used by the fairies to make all weathers.
Climate chaos I have planned
On Earth, and here, in Fairyland!

Contents

A Misty Morning

"Wake up, sleepy head!" cried Kirsty Tate to her friend, Rachel, as she jumped out of bed and started to dress.

Rachel Walker was asleep in the spare bed in Kirsty's room. She was staying with Kirsty and her parents in the village of Wetherbury. Sleepily, she rolled over and opened her eyes. "I was dreaming

that we were back in Fairyland," she told Kirsty. "The weather was topsy-turvy – sunny and snowing all at the same time – and Doodle was trying to sort it out." Doodle, the fairies' magic weather cockerel, had been on Rachel's mind a lot lately, because she and Kirsty were on an important fairy mission!

Each day in Fairyland, with the help of the Weather Fairies, Doodle used his magic tail feathers to organise the weather. Each of the seven magic feathers controlled a different kind of weather, and each of the seven Weather Fairies was responsible for working with one feather in particular. The system worked perfectly until mean old Jack Frost sent seven goblins to steal Doodle's magic feathers.

The goblins ran off into the human world with one feather each, and when poor Doodle followed them out of Fairyland, he found himself transformed into a rusty metal weather-vane. The Queen of the Fairies had asked Rachel and Kirsty to help find the magic feathers and return them to Doodle.

11

Meanwhile, Fairyland's weather was all mixed up – and the goblins had been using the feathers to cause weather chaos in the human world too.

"Poor Doodle," Kirsty said, looking out of the window at the old barn where the cockerel was perched. Her dad had found Doodle lying in the park, and thinking he was an ordinary weather-vane, Mr Tate had brought him home and put him on the barn roof.

"Hopefully we'll find another magic feather today," Kirsty continued. "We've already found four of the stolen feathers. We just need to find the other three and then Doodle will get his magic back."

"Yes," Rachel agreed, brightening at the thought. "But I have to go home in three days, so we don't have long!" As she gazed out at the blue sky, a wisp of silvery mist caught her eye. "Look, that cloud is shaped just like a feather!" she said.

Kirsty looked where Rachel was pointing. "I can't see anything."

Rachel looked again. The wispy shape had vanished. "Perhaps I imagined it," she sighed, turning away to dress.

The memory of the dream fizzed in her tummy like lemonade bubbles.

It felt like a magical start to the day.

She loved staying with Kirsty and sharing fairy adventures with her. The girls had met whilst on holiday on Rainspell Island with their parents.

That was when they had first helped the fairies. On that occasion, Jack Frost had cast a nasty spell to banish the Rainbow Fairies from Fairyland, and the girls had helped all seven of them get safely home.

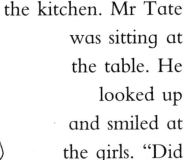

Rachel and Kirsty hurried down to the kitchen. Mr Tate was sitting at the table. He looked up and smiled at the girls. "Did you sleep well?"

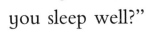

"Yes, thanks," Rachel replied. As she sat down, she saw a bright green notice on the kitchen table. It read, Grand Fun Run at Green Wood Forest, Wetherbury. Everyone welcome. She looked at the date. "That's today."

"Yes. Mum's running in it," said Kirsty.

"Most of the village is taking part. Why don't you two go and watch?" suggested Mr Tate. "You could give Mum some moral support."

"OK," Rachel and Kirsty agreed happily.

Maybe we could look for goblins on
the way, thought Rachel. She felt excited,
and a bit nervous. Goblins were nasty,
tricky things and Jack Frost had cast a
spell to make them bigger than normal.
Thankfully, fairy law states that nothing
can be taller than the King and Queen's
fairy castle, so the goblins couldn't get
too big. But they still stood nearly as
high as Rachel and Kirsty's shoulders.

Mr Tate finished his cup of tea and
stood up. "I'm going to pick up Gran
and take her to watch the fun run. We
might see you there," he told the girls.

"OK, Dad. Goodbye," Kirsty said
with a wave.

Just then, Mrs Tate dashed into the
kitchen, wearing her jogging kit of
shorts, T-shirt and trainers. She smiled at

Kirsty and Rachel.
"Sorry, I can't stop,
girls. I promised to
help mark out the
course in the forest."

"That's all right,
Mum. We'll follow
you up there," Kirsty said.

"We're coming to cheer you on,"
Rachel explained.

"See you at the woods then!" Mrs Tate
called cheerfully as she disappeared out
of the door.

A little later, Kirsty and Rachel set out
for Green Wood Forest themselves.

"Let's take the river path," Kirsty suggested.
"It's a bit longer, but it's much prettier."

"Oh, yes, we might see some ducklings,"
Rachel agreed eagerly.

As the girls walked up Twisty Lane, sunlight poured through the dancing tree branches and spots of light speckled the road like golden coins. Soon they reached the river. It was very pretty down by the water, where cheerful buttercups dotted the grass and cows grazed happily.

Rachel spotted little puffs of mist rising from the water. "Look! Do you think that could be fairy mist?" she asked.

"I'm not sure," Kirsty replied. "There's often mist round water, isn't there?"

"Oh, yes, especially in the morning and the evening," Rachel remembered. She felt a little disappointed, but brightened when she saw two swans gliding past, followed by three young cygnets. Dragonflies with gossamer wings perched in the reeds beside the sparkling river. "It's a perfect day!" she remarked.

Kirsty nodded. Just ahead she could see the start of the forest. Something was shimmering on a branch of one of the nearer trees. It looked like a ragged silver-grey shawl, glimmering softly in the sunlight.

"What's that?" she asked Rachel.

Rachel went over to have a look. "I don't know, but it's lovely!" she replied. "Just like angel hair for decorating trees at Christmas."

"There's lots more of it on the other branches. Isn't it pretty?" Kirsty touched a strand of the strange, silvery stuff. It clung to her fingers for a moment, before melting away. "It feels cold!" Kirsty shivered, rubbing her hands together.

Rachel leaned forward for a closer look. Tiny silvery lights shimmered among the fine, silky threads. "I'm sure this is fairy mist," she whispered excitedly.

Kirsty's eyes lit up. "I think you're right," she agreed. She looked towards a clump of tall oaks. A wispy cloud of the strange sparkly mist was building in the sky and floating gently down towards the trees. "More fairy mist!" Kirsty pointed out. "Come on!"

Magic in the Mist

The girls ran towards a stile that led
into the wood. They were out of breath
by the time they jumped down onto the
forest path and looked around. Wispy,
silver mist clung to trees everywhere
and coated the grass with tiny droplets.
Every twig, leaf and flower glowed
and shimmered with a soft silver light.

And where the sunbeams reached down through the trees, the fairy mist sparkled with rainbow light.

"Oh!" breathed Rachel. "It's so beautiful!"

Kirsty stared open-mouthed at the forest. It looked almost as magical as Fairyland itself!

Slowly, the girls moved forward.

After a few steps, Rachel realised that she couldn't see very far ahead.

"This mist is building up fast," she said. "The goblin with the Mist Feather must be hiding really nearby."

Kirsty nodded as thick fog swirled around them. "You're right, Rachel," she agreed. "And we can hardly see a thing. The goblin could be right behind us!"

Rachel rubbed her bare arms and shivered nervously. Only a couple of minutes had passed, but as the mist grew thicker, the forest began to feel dark and unfriendly. Nothing glittered or gleamed anymore. The fog was settling around the girls like a cold blanket.

Shadowy figures moved up ahead. A man wearing a red T-shirt ran out in front of the girls as another runner  burst out of the trees. They were heading straight for each other. "Watch out!" called Kirsty. But it was too late. Crash! The runners bumped into each other.

"Sorry. Didn't see you there!" one
of them said, rubbing his head.

"I've never seen fog like this in
summer," replied the other one.

Rachel and Kirsty could hear rustles
and bumps all round them. Complaining
voices echoed through the fog. Lots of
runners were getting lost and having
to walk in order to avoid the trees.

"What a shame. This fog is ruining the fun run," said Rachel.

The fog still seemed to be getting thicker. It cloaked the trees in robes of dull grey, making them look dark and sinister.

Suddenly, something caught Kirsty's eye. "Over there!" she pointed.

A bright light was moving towards them, shining like a lantern. Soon the girls could see that it was a tiny gleaming fairy.

"Oh!" gasped Kirsty. "It's Evie the Mist Fairy!"

"Hello again, Rachel and Kirsty," cried Evie in a bright, tinkly voice, as she hovered in the air in front of them. The girls had met Evie in Fairyland, along with all the other Weather Fairies. She had long dark hair and violet eyes. She wore a floaty lilac dress with purple boots, and her wand had a sparkly silver tip from which wisps of shimmering mist drifted constantly.

"Oh, we're so glad to see you!" said Rachel delightedly.

"We really need your help," Kirsty added. "We're sure that the goblin with the Mist Feather isn't far away."

"Yes!" agreed Evie, a frown on her tiny face. "And he's causing lots of misty mischief!"

29

"Could you leave a magic trail behind us, as we go further into the woods?" Rachel asked. "Then we can look for the goblin and still find our way back to the stile and out."

Evie grinned. She waved her wand and a fountain of fairy dust shot out. It floated to the ground and formed a glittering path. "Of course, now we won't get lost!" she said. "But we might bump into the runners," Kirsty pointed out. "Let's turn ourselves into fairies, Rachel, then we can fly."

The Fairy Queen had given Rachel and Kirsty beautiful golden lockets full of fairy dust. The girls sprinkled themselves with the magic dust and soon shrank to fairy size. The trees seemed as big as giants' castles looming out of the thick fog.

"I love being a fairy!" Kirsty sang out happily.

Rachel twisted round to look over her shoulder. There were her fairy wings on her back, shining and delicate.

"Hooray!" Evie rose into the air, a trail of glittering mist streaming from her wand, and the two girls followed her deeper into the forest.

Below them, the runners were still stumbling about in the fog. "Poor Mum. She was really looking forward to today. That nasty goblin's spoiling everyone's fun," said Kirsty crossly.

Suddenly, Rachel spotted a dark, hunched shape in the mist below. She waved urgently to Kirsty and Evie. "Look down there," she called softly. "I think we've found the goblin!"

Goblin in the Fog

They all floated down to investigate. The mist was heavier here and sticky. It dragged at Rachel's wings as she flew through it. "Oh, it's not a goblin – it's just a dead tree," she sighed, landing on the thick twisted trunk. She felt disappointed. The dark, squat shape had looked just like a goblin from the air.

35

"We may not have found him yet,"
Kirsty whispered to her friend, "but I still
think that goblin's nearby. The mist here
smells nasty and musty and it's harder to
fly through."

Rachel fluttered her beautiful shiny wings.
"Yes," she agreed. "It's like cold porridge."

Just then, they heard a gruff, complaining
voice. "It's not fair! I'm cold and I'm lost
and I'm hungry!" There was a loud sniff,
like a pig snorting. "Poor me!"

Rachel, Kirsty, and Evie looked at each
other in excitement.

"That's definitely a goblin speaking!" declared Evie.

"Quick! Let's hide in that tree before he sees us," suggested Rachel.

They flew upwards to land on the branch of a huge oak and peered down through the thick green leaves. Sure enough, the goblin sat on a log below them. They could see the top of his head and his enormous bony feet. They could also hear a horrible gurgling sound, like slimy stuff going down a plughole.

37

"Lost in this horrible forest! And I'm so hungry," moaned the goblin, clutching his rumbling tummy. "I'd love some toadstool stew and worm dumplings!" Suddenly he jumped up.

"What was that? Who's there?" He peered up into the tree's branches. Rachel, Kirsty and Evie quickly darted behind the oak leaves and after a moment the goblin sank down onto his log again. "Must have been a squirrel," he muttered. "I want to go home!"

The girls could see the goblin clearly now. He had bulging, crossed eyes and a big, lumpy nose like a potato.

His arms were long and skinny but he had short legs and knobbly knees.

"Look what he's holding!" whispered Evie.

Kirsty and Rachel peered through the leaves and saw that a beautiful silvery feather with a lilac tip was clutched in the goblin's stubby fingers. "The Mist Feather!" the girls exclaimed together.

Then Rachel frowned. "If the goblin's lost in the fog, why doesn't he use the magic feather to get rid of it?" she asked.

"Because he doesn't know how," Evie explained. "He's waving the feather about all over the place without thinking – but by doing so he's only making more and more mist."

It was true. The goblin was shaking the Mist Feather and mumbling to himself sorrowfully as thick swirls of fog drifted around him. "Earwig fritters, beetle pancakes, lovely slug sandwiches…" he muttered.

Just then, one of the runners passed close by. The goblin shot to his feet and hid behind a tree. He was trembling so much that the three friends could hear his knees knocking together. "It's a…it's a Pogwurzel!" he whispered in panic.

As the sound of the runner's footsteps faded, the goblin peeped out. "Phew! The Pogwurzel's gone." He flopped back down on the log, but carried on looking about him nervously.

Kirsty turned to Evie. "What is a Pogwurzel?" she asked.

Evie smiled, her violet eyes sparkling. "Pogwurzels are strange, magical, goblin-chasing monsters!" she replied.

Rachel looked at the fairy curiously. "Where do they live?" She and Kirsty had been to Fairyland a few times now. They had seen elves, goblins and all kinds of fairies – but never a Pogwurzel.

Evie gave a peal of silvery laughter. "Nowhere!" she said. "Because they don't exist! You see goblin children can be really naughty, so their mothers tell them that if they don't do as they're told, a Pogwurzel will come and chase them!"

Kirsty and Rachel laughed so much they nearly fell off the branch.

Then Rachel suddenly turned to Kirsty and Evie in excitement. "I've got an idea," she whispered, her eyes shining. "I think I know how we can get the Mist Feather back!"

The Pogwurzel Plot

Evie and Kirsty stared at Rachel. "Tell us!" they pleaded.

Rachel outlined her plan. "If we can convince the goblin that the forest is full of Pogwurzels, he'll do anything to escape. He's bound to want the mist cleared away, so he can find his way out of the wood.

Since he's too stupid to work out how to use the Mist Feather to clear the fog, maybe we can persuade him to give the feather to Evie and let her try."

Evie clapped her hands together in delight. "Then I can keep it and take it back to Doodle!" she said. "It's a brilliant plan!"

"But I'm not sure how we can make the goblin think that there are hundreds of Pogwurzels in the forest," Rachel added.

The three friends racked their brains. Kirsty thought of her mum and the other runners trying to find their way around the fun run course. That gave her an idea of her own. "I know just how we can convince the goblin about Pogwurzels," she cried. "Evie, if you make us human-sized again, Rachel and I can creep up on the goblin from behind, then run past him, screaming that a Pogwurzel is chasing us!"

"Yes, that could work," Evie agreed.

"We'll have to be very convincing," Rachel put in.

Evie nodded. "But you two can do it.
I know you can," she said encouragingly.
The three friends flew silently down to
the ground behind the oak tree. Evie
waved her wand and the
girls zoomed up to
their normal height.
"Ready?" asked Kirsty.
"You bet," Rachel
replied firmly.
The girls crept
towards the goblin.
They could see
him sitting on
his log, still
muttering to himself.
"Now!" hissed Rachel.
Kirsty dashed forward. "Help! Help!
Save us from the Pogwurzel!" she shouted.

48

Rachel ran after her. "It's huge and scary and won't leave us alone!" she cried.

The goblin leapt to his feet, his eyes like saucers. "What?" he gasped. "Who are you?"

Kirsty stopped. "Oh, my goodness, a goblin in Pogwurzel Wood!" she exclaimed, pretending to be surprised.

Rachel stopped too. "You must be very brave," she declared.

The goblin's crossed-eyes flicked from Rachel to Kirsty. "Why?" he demanded shakily. "Are their many Pogwurzels around here?"

"Oh, yes," Kirsty chimed in. "Hundreds. This forest is full of them. One of them was chasing us just now," she added, looking nervously over her shoulder. "He'll be along soon I should think."

Just then, Evie fluttered down, her wings shining in the fog. "Pogwurzels especially love to catch goblins, you know. I've heard that they cook them and eat them," she said.

"Eat them!" the goblin's face turned pale with fear.

"Oh, yes. If I was you, I'd get out of this wood right now," Evie went on.

"But I can't," wailed the goblin. "I've lost my way. The fog is so thick I can hardly see my own bony toes!"

Evie smiled. "I'll help you," she said sweetly. "Just give me that feather you're holding and I'll magic a clear pathway out of the forest for you."

Kirsty and Rachel hardly dared breathe. Their plan was working so far, but what would the goblin do next?

He pinched his nose thoughtfully. "I don't know. Jack Frost won't like it if I give you the Mist Feather."

"But he's not the one being chased by a Pogwurzel, is he?" Rachel pointed out quickly. "He's not the one who'll be roasted and toasted and turned into Goblin Pie!"

"The Pogwurzels in this wood are extra-enormous," Kirsty put in. "And really, really fierce."

"So is Jack Frost," the goblin said, looking sullen. "I think I'll keep the feather."

Kirsty's heart sank. It looked like the goblin was more stubborn than they had expected. She exchanged looks with Rachel. Now what could they do?

Goblin Pie

Evie hovered close to the girls. "I've got an idea," she whispered. "You distract the goblin, so he won't notice what I'm doing."

"What are you all talking about?" demanded the goblin suspiciously.

"We think we heard another Pogwurzel," Kirsty replied.

"Where?" the goblin spun round anxiously.

While his back was turned, Evie waved her wand in a complicated pattern. A big fountain of silver and violet sparks shot into a nearby bush, carrying fairy magic there.

"I can hear it! It's coming this way!" Rachel called to the goblin.

"Don't believe you," the goblin sneered. "I can't hear it. You're just trying to scare me. I bet you never even saw a Pogwurzel in the first place."

"Listen properly for yourself then," Evie said.

The goblin put his head on one side and frowned in concentration. Kirsty and Rachel waited. They weren't sure exactly what Evie had planned.

Suddenly a deep, scary roar came from the centre of the nearby bush.

"Raaghh! I'm a ferocious Pogwurzel! And I really fancy Goblin Pie for my supper!"

"Wow! Evie's magical voice is really scary," Kirsty whispered to Rachel.

The goblin stiffened. "Help me, Mummy!" he cried. "A Pogwurzel wants to eat me! I'm sorry I put those toenail clippings in your bed. I won't do it again. Help!" He stumbled behind Kirsty and Rachel, trying to hide. "Don't eat me, Mr Pogwurzel. Eat these girls

instead. I bet they taste sweeter than me!"
Evie's magical trick voice came from
the bush again. "I only eat
goblins," it boomed.
"Especially really
naughty ones
– like you!"
The goblin
squealed in
alarm and his
eyes bulged.
He took the
Mist Feather
from his belt and
thrust it at Evie.
"Make the mist go
away so I can get out of
here," he begged. "I don't
want to be made into Goblin Pie!"

Evie gave a joyful smile, took the
feather and waved it expertly in the air.
A clear path immediately appeared
through the mist. The goblin gave a
final terrified glance over his shoulder
and then ran away as fast as he could,
his big feet flapping noisily.

Kirsty, Rachel and Evie laughed merrily.

"Evie, that trick voice was brilliant!"
Rachel said.

"It even scared me!" laughed Kirsty.

"And now we have the Mist Feather!"
Evie declared, waving it over her head.

Silver sparks shot into the air and the mist began to fade. Moments later, the sun shone down onto the forest again.

Rachel and Kirsty beamed. "We can give another magic feather back to Doodle!" Rachel said happily.

Evie flew up and did a little twirl in the air for joy. Silver and violet mist sparkled all around her.

"And the fun run should be easier going now," Kirsty put in. "Let's go and see if we can spot Mum before we head home to Doodle."

Back on Course

The three friends made their way towards the fun run course.

The bracken and forest paths were touched with gold, and the smell of earth and green leaves filled the air. Runners pounded along between trees marked with big red signs. Everyone could see where they were going now.

"You'd better hide on my shoulder," Rachel said to Evie.

Evie nodded and fluttered beneath Rachel's hair.

Suddenly, Kirsty spotted her mum dashing through the trees. Two other runners were close on her heels.

"Come on, Mum!" Kirsty shouted.

"You can do it!" yelled Rachel.

Kirsty's mum threw them a brief smile and waved. "Not far to go now," she called.

Kirsty and Rachel jumped up and down with delight. Evie cheered too, but only Rachel could hear her silvery voice.

"Looks like your mum's doing well," said a voice at Kirsty's side.

"Dad! Gran! You're here!" Kirsty exclaimed.

"Only just in time. That fog held us up," said Mr Tate. "Strange how it's completely disappeared now. Almost like magic."

Rachel and Kirsty looked at each other and smiled.

"We're going to head home now," Kirsty told her dad.

"Right you are," he replied. "We'll go and wait for Mum at the finish line."

On the way home, the girls revelled in the glorious sunshine, but Kirsty couldn't help missing the sparkly fairy mist just a little bit.

"Time to give Doodle his feather back," said Rachel, as they reached Kirsty's cottage. "I wonder if he'll speak to us again." Every time the girls had returned a tail feather, Doodle had sprung briefly to life and started to speak. He'd given them part of a message and they were keen to hear the rest.

"I hope so," said Kirsty. She repeated what Doodle had said so far. "Beware! Jack Frost will come…"

Evie flew up to the barn roof. As she slotted the feather into place, the girls watched eagerly.

A fountain of copper and gold sparks fizzed from Doodle's tail. The rusty old weather-vane disappeared and in its place blazed a fiery magic cockerel. Doodle fluffed up his glorious feathers and turned to stare at Rachel and Kirsty. "If his—" he squawked. But before he could finish the message, his feathers turned to iron and he became an ordinary weather-vane again.

Kirsty frowned. "Beware! Jack Frost will come if his…" she said, putting together all the words Doodle had said so far.

"Jack Frost will come if his what?" queried Rachel curiously.

Kirsty shook her head. "We'll just have to find the next feather and hope Doodle can tell us," she sighed.

Evie nodded. "It's important to know the whole message. Jack Frost is dangerous," she warned. "And now I must leave you." She hugged Rachel and Kirsty in turn. "Dear friends. Thank you for helping me."

"You're welcome," said Kirsty.

"Say hello to all our friends in Fairyland for us," added Rachel.

"I will," Evie promised, as she zoomed up into the brilliant blue sky. Her wand fizzed trails of silver mist, then she was gone.

Kirsty chuckled. "I've just remembered something the goblin said. I wonder whose toenail clippings he put in his mum's bed!" she said.

Rachel laughed happily. What an exciting day it had been and there were still two days of her holiday left!

Win Rainbow Magic Goodies!

There are lots of Rainbow Magic fairies, and we want to know which one is your favourite! Send us a picture of her and tell us in thirty words why she is your favourite and why you like Rainbow Magic books. Each month we will put the entries into a draw and select one winner to receive a Rainbow Magic Sparkly T-shirt and Goody Bag!

Send your entry on a postcard to Rainbow Magic Competition, Orchard Books, 338 Euston Road, London NW1 3BH.
Australian readers should email: childrens.books@hachette.com.au
New Zealand readers should write to Rainbow Magic Competition, 4 Whetu Place, Mairangi Bay, Auckland NZ.
Don't forget to include your name and address.
Only one entry per child.

Good luck!

RAINBOW magic

The Weather Fairies

Crystal, Abigail, Pearl, Goldie and
Evie have got their feathers back.
Now Rachel and Kirsty must help
Storm the Lightning Fairy

Magic in the Air

"I can't believe tomorrow is my last day here," groaned Rachel Walker. She was staying for a week's holiday with her friend, Kirsty Tate, at the Tates' house in Wetherbury. The girls had had so many adventures together, they knew it was going to be difficult to say goodbye.

They were walking to the park, keen to get outside now the rain had stopped. It had been pouring down all night, but now the sun was shining.

"Put your coats on, though, won't

you?" Mrs Tate had told them before they set off. "It looks quite breezy out there."

"It's been such fun, having you to stay," Kirsty told her friend. "I don't think I'll ever forget this week, will you?"

Rachel shook her head. "No way," she agreed firmly.

The two friends smiled at each other. It had been a very busy week. A snowy, windy, cloudy, sunny, misty week – thanks to Jack Frost and his naughty goblins. The goblins had stolen the seven magic tail feathers from Doodle, the Fairyland weather cockerel, and taken one each into the human world. The feathers were used by the Weather Fairies to control the weather so the goblins were stirring up all kinds of trouble!

Rachel and Kirsty were helping the Weather Fairies to get the feathers back. Without them, Doodle was just an ordinary iron weather-vane! Kirsty's dad had found him lying in the park after he'd chased the goblins into the human world. Mr Tate had brought him home and put him on the roof of the old barn.

"Doodle's got five of his magic feathers back now. But I do hope we find the last two before you have to go home," Kirsty said, pushing open the park gates.

Rachel nodded, but before she could say anything, there was a pattering sound and raindrops started splashing down.

The girls looked up in dismay to see a
huge purple storm cloud covering the sun.
The sky was darkening by the second and
the rain was falling more and more
heavily.

"Quick!" Kirsty shouted. "Before we get
soaked!"

The girls started to run, and Rachel put
her hands over her head as raindrops
pelted them from all sides. She could
hardly see the path ahead through the
sudden downpour. "Where are we
going?" she yelled.

"Let's just find some shelter," Kirsty
replied, grabbing Rachel's hand and
pulling her along. "I'm soaked through
already!"

The girls stopped under a large chestnut
tree near the park entrance. The tree's

wide, leafy branches gave good cover.
"Great idea," shivered Rachel, trying to
shake the raindrops from her coat.

But just as she said that, there was a
deafening rumble of thunder, followed
by an almighty FLASH! The whole sky
was lit up by a blast of lightning.
Kirsty and Rachel watched in alarm as
a lightning bolt slammed straight into
the chestnut.

"We need to get away from here
quickly," Kirsty cried, jumping back in
fright. "It's dangerous being under the
trees in a thunder storm!"

"Wait a minute," Rachel said, staring
at the branch. Rain was pouring off her
shoulders but she didn't seem to notice.
"Kirsty, look. The branch is *sparkling*."

And so it was. The leaves were

shining a bright, glittering green, glowing against the darkness of the day. Tiny twinkling lights were flickering all over the bark of the branch. It reminded Kirsty of the trees they'd seen in Fairyland – the way they almost seemed to sparkle with fairy dust. And that made her think that maybe...

"It's a *magical* storm!" Kirsty exclaimed in delight, her eyes almost as bright as the shining leaves. "Look at the sky, Rachel!"

Have you checked out the

RAINBOW
magic®

website at:

www.rainbowmagic.co.uk

RAINBOW magic

The Twilight Fairies

Special thanks
to Narinder Dhami

ORCHARD BOOKS
338 Euston Road, London NW1 3BH
Orchard Books Australia
Level 17/207 Kent Street, Sydney, NSW 2000
A Paperback Original

First published in 2010 by Orchard Books

HiT entertainment

A CIP catalogue record for this book is available
from the British Library.

ISBN 978 1 40830 908 7

1 3 5 7 9 10 8 6 4 2

Printed in China by Imago

The paper and board used in this paperback are natural recyclable
products made from wood grown in sustainable forests. The
manufacturing processes conform to the environmental regulations
of the country of origin.

Orchard Books is a division of Hachette Children's Books,
an Hachette UK company

www.hachette.co.uk

Zara

the Starlight Fairy

by Daisy Meadows

ORCHARD BOOKS

www.rainbowmagic.co.uk

The Fairyland Palace

Observatory

Games Area

Fairy Homes

Ferry

CAMP STAR GAZE

Mirror Lake

The Twinkling Tree

Starry Glade

The Twilight Fairies' magical powers
Bring harmony to the night-time hours.
But now their magic belongs to me,
And I'll cause chaos, you shall see!

Sunset, moonlight and starlight too,
There'll be no more sweet dreams for you,
From evening dusk to morning light
I am the master of the night!

Contents

A Star is Born!

"This telescope is huge, Kirsty!" Rachel Walker said excitedly to her best friend, Kirsty Tate. "I can't wait to have a look at the night sky."

"It's going to be amazing," Kirsty agreed as they stared up at the enormous silver telescope.

The girls were spending a week of the

summer holidays with their parents at Camp Stargaze, which had its very own observatory for studying the stars. The observatory was a square white building topped with a large dome, and charts and pictures of the night sky hung on the walls. In the middle of the observatory stood the gigantic telescope, and Professor Hetty, the camp astronomer, was explaining to Rachel, Kirsty and the other children about the stars and constellations.

"As you know, this area was chosen for Camp Stargaze because we can get really clear views of the night sky from here," Professor Hetty reminded them. She was a jolly, round-faced woman with twinkling blue eyes and a mop of red hair.

"Have any of you ever done a join-the-dots puzzle?"

Everyone nodded.

"Well, a constellation is rather like a join-the-dots puzzle!" Professor Hetty explained with a smile. "A constellation is made of individual stars that join up to make a picture, just like the puzzle. But although the stars look close together to us here on earth, sometimes they're actually millions of miles apart! Let's take a look, shall we?"

Professor Hetty pressed a button on the wall. There was a noise overhead,

and Rachel and Kirsty glanced up to see
a large section of the domed roof slide
smoothly back. This revealed the dark,
velvety night sky and sparkling silver stars
twinkling here and there like diamonds
in a jewellery box. Everyone gasped
and applauded.
"Wonderful!"
Professor
Hetty said
eagerly.
"I never get
tired of looking
at the night sky.
It's so magical."

Rachel nudged Kirsty.
"Professor Hetty doesn't know just
how magical the night-time really is!"
she whispered.

Kirsty smiled. When she and Rachel
had arrived at Camp Stargaze, Ava the
Sunset Fairy had rushed from Fairyland to
ask for their help. The girls had discovered
that Ava and the other six Twilight Fairies
made sure the hours from dusk to dawn
were peaceful and happy, with the help
of their satin bags of magical fairy dust.

But while the Twilight Fairies were
enjoying a party under the stars with their
fairy friends, Jack Frost had broken into
the Fairyland Palace with his naughty
goblin servants. The goblins had stolen
the magical bags that were hidden under
the Twilight Fairies' pillows. Then, with
a wave of his ice wand, Jack Frost had
sent the goblins and the bags spinning
away from Fairyland to hide in the
human world. Jack Frost's plan was to

cause night-time chaos for both fairies and humans, but Rachel, Kirsty and the Twilight Fairies were determined not to let that happen.

"I wonder if we'll meet another Twilight Fairy today?" Kirsty murmured to Rachel as they all lined up to have a look through the telescope. "I'm so glad we managed to find Ava's and Lexi's magical bags, but we still have five more to go!"

"Remember, we have to let the magic come to us," Rachel reminded her.

The girls' new friend, Alex, was first to use the telescope, and Professor Hetty showed her how to look through the eyepiece. Alex peered into the telescope eagerly.

"Everything looks so close!" she gasped.

"Can you see any pictures in the stars,

Alex?" asked Professor Hetty.

"I think I see something…" Alex peered more closely. "Oh!" She burst out laughing. "I can see a constellation shaped like a toothbrush!"

"Well done," said Professor Hetty. "And those of you who aren't using the telescope should be able to see it too, if you look hard."

Rachel and Kirsty gazed intently up at the sky.

"Oh, there it is!" Kirsty exclaimed, pointing out the toothbrush of stars to Rachel. "And it even has bristles!"

"Lucas, it's your turn," Professor Hetty said.

Lucas, another of Rachel and Kirsty's friends, took Alex's place at the telescope. He studied the sky for a few minutes and then turned to Professor Hetty.

"That constellation near the toothbrush looks like a pair of pyjamas," he said with a grin.

"Right again!" Professor Hetty smiled. "Did you spot the slipper constellation too, just below the pyjamas, Lucas?"

Lucas looked again. "Yes, I can see it now," he said. "It really is like a join-the-dots puzzle!"

It was Rachel's turn after Lucas had finished.

"I'll just change the angle of the

telescope a little, Rachel," Professor Hetty told her. "Then you should be able to spot something different."

Rachel peered through the glass eyepiece. At first she got a shock because the stars looked so close and were so bright. Then, as her eyesight adjusted, she saw the constellation shaped like a slipper that Professor Hetty had mentioned earlier.

"This is amazing!" Rachel gasped.

"Can you see any other constellations, Rachel?" Professor Hetty asked.

Rachel stared at the night sky. For a moment she couldn't see anything new, and then all of a sudden she noticed that some of the stars seemed to be grouped together in the outline of a face. The face had spiky hair and a spiky beard as well as a pointy nose.

"I think I see a face," Rachel said hesitantly.

"A face?" Professor Hetty sounded very surprised. "I wasn't expecting that!" And she gazed up at the night sky, trying to spot it for herself. Meanwhile, Rachel was frowning. That face in the stars looked familiar…

"Aha, I see it now!" Professor Hetty exclaimed. "And look, everyone – a star has drifted away from the toothbrush constellation to join up with the face. We're actually seeing a new constellation forming in front of our very eyes. How amazing! I've never seen anything like it!"

"Kirsty, look at this!" Rachel said quickly, moving aside to let her friend take her place at the telescope.

Kirsty took a good look at the

constellation as the drifting star settled into its new place, becoming part of the face's spiky beard. Her eyes widened as she realised exactly who it was.

It was Jack Frost!

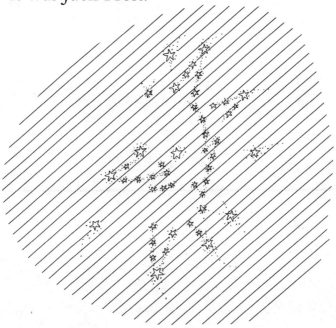

Zara Zooms In

"Surely Jack Frost's face can't be a real constellation?" Kirsty murmured to Rachel as they followed Professor Hetty and the others out of the observatory.

"Well, Professor Hetty seems to think it is!" Rachel replied. The professor was so excited by the new constellation that she hadn't stopped talking about it. "But we know that Jack Frost must be using the Twilight Fairies' magic to create havoc in the night sky."

Outside the observatory Peter, one of the camp leaders, was waiting to introduce the evening activity. Immediately Professor Hetty began telling him about the new constellation.

"And look, Peter, some stars are moving across from the other constellations to join it!" she explained.

Rachel and Kirsty glanced upwards. Several more stars had detached themselves from the pyjamas constellation that Lucas had spotted earlier, and were floating across the sky. As the girls watched, the stars positioned themselves on Jack Frost's face, forming his familiar, icy grin.

"Right, everyone, we're going to do some orienteering this evening," Peter told them.

There was a murmur of excitement.

"Oh, great," said Kirsty. "We did orienteering when we stayed at that adventure camp, didn't we, Rachel?"

Rachel nodded. "It's fun," she agreed. "And it'll give us a chance to look around and try to find out what Jack Frost is up to!" she added in a low voice.

"First, get into pairs, and I'll give you a map of the constellations and a compass," Peter went on. "You

should use them to find three locations within the camp, and each location name is the clue to a puzzle. Then, when you get to the last location, there's a surprise waiting!"

"But you'll have to be quick," Professor Hetty called as she and Peter began handing out the compasses and maps. "This is a great night to be out under the stars because we can watch this new constellation forming. But if you take too long, more stars will have moved, and you may not be able to find your way!"

Kirsty looked up at the night sky again. The outline of Jack Frost now had a neck and the beginning of shoulders.

"At this rate there won't be any constellations left in the sky except Jack Frost!" she told Rachel.

Rachel looked dismayed. "That would be awful!" she exclaimed, as her eye was caught by another sparkling star floating across the dark sky.

But this time the star didn't join the Jack Frost constellation. Instead it suddenly plunged down towards the earth, leaving a trail of golden sparks behind it like a firework. Rachel clutched Kirsty's arm.

"Kirsty, I think that might be a shooting star!" she gasped.

As the two girls watched, the star spiralled downwards and disappeared behind the observatory. No one else had noticed because they were too busy studying their maps.

Kirsty and Rachel slipped away quietly and ran to the observatory, their hearts thumping with excitement.

"Girls," called a clear, tinkling voice, "I'm over here!" And suddenly a tiny fairy popped out from behind the observatory.

"It's Zara the Starlight Fairy!" Rachel said.

"Hello, Zara," said Kirsty. "Welcome to Camp Stargaze!"

Zara smiled as the girls rushed over to her. She wore an oversized T-shirt scattered with stars,

black leggings and silver shoes, as well as a silver star bracelet and matching necklace.

"Yes, it's me, girls," she replied. "And I'm sure you've noticed that Jack Frost is using my magical star dust to move all the stars around?"

Kirsty and Rachel nodded.

"Jack Frost is so vain, he wants a big picture of himself in the sky every single night!" Zara explained.

"So he's stealing stars and ruining all the beautiful constellations. That means ships won't be able to navigate at sea, and birds which fly at night and use the stars to find their way will get lost, too. It'll be chaos! My bag of star dust is around here somewhere, so will you help me find it and stop Jack Frost?"

"Of course we will!" Rachel and Kirsty cried.

Scattered Star Dust

"Thank you, girls," Zara said gratefully.

"We can look for your bag of star dust while we search for the three mystery locations," Rachel pointed out, switching on her torch and shining it onto the map.

"To find the first location, go north, and mind you don't slip!" Kirsty read out. She placed the compass on the map and the three friends watched the needle swing around and point north.

"Mind you don't slip…" Rachel repeated thoughtfully, looking up at the stars. "Oh! I think that means the first place we have to find is right underneath the slipper constellation. That's north from where we're standing."

"Luckily, the slipper still has most of its stars, so let's go right away," Zara suggested.

Quickly Zara flew down to perch on Kirsty's shoulder, hiding behind her hair. Then the girls set off towards the slipper constellation. The other children, including Alex and Lucas, were still studying their maps, staring at the stars and trying to work out how to use the compass. But then Rachel noticed two boys wearing baggy T-shirts, shorts and baseball caps also heading off in the direction of the slipper constellation. They barged rudely past Alex and Lucas, knocking the map from Lucas's hand.

"Hey, watch out!" Lucas called. But the two boys didn't stop.

"Looks like those boys have worked out where the first location is, too," Rachel remarked as she and Kirsty made their way through the tents.

Suddenly, there was the sound of twittering overhead. Surprised, Rachel and Kirsty glanced up and saw a flock of beautiful, bright blue birds flying above them.

The birds were tweeting miserably, turning their heads as if they were searching for something.

"Oh no!" Zara gasped, popping out from behind Kirsty's hair. "This is exactly what I told you would happen, girls. These birds are Blue Buntings and they fly at night, using the stars to find their way. They're completely lost!"

"Poor things," said Kirsty as the birds flew on, still chirping sadly to each other. "We must find your bag of magical dust and put the stars back in the right place, Zara."

Zara nodded. "We're almost right

underneath the slipper constellation now, girls," she pointed out.

Rachel was shining her torch just ahead of them. "I can see something between the tents!" she said. "It's a signpost and it has a number '1' on it."

"Well done, girls!" Zara exclaimed. "You've found the first location. And just in time, too…"

Rachel and Kirsty looked up at the slipper constellation, and saw several more stars slide away to make up the outline of one of Jack Frost's arms.

"I hope everyone else manages to find it too," Kirsty said anxiously. "There's hardly any of the slipper left now."

"There's something glowing at the bottom of the signpost," Rachel said. "I wonder what it is?"

"We saw it first!" yelled a voice behind them.

Zara rushed to hide again as two boys ran out of the shadows and pushed roughly past them. Rachel recognised them as the same boys who'd barged Alex and Lucas out of the way earlier.

"Look, prizes!" one of them shouted gleefully. "And they're all for US!"

Rachel and Kirsty could see now that there was a pile of glow-in-the-dark star stickers heaped at the bottom of the signpost.

"You shouldn't take them all," Rachel called as the two boys grabbed the stickers. "I think they're meant for everyone."

The boys ignored her and began sticking the stars all over themselves.

Then, shrieking with glee, they ran off.

"That wasn't very nice of them, was it?" Kirsty sighed as the two boys, glowing all over with stars, disappeared from sight again. "What's the next clue, Rachel?"

Rachel looked at the map again. "To find the second location, go west and brush up on your orienteering skills!" she read out.

"West is that way," Kirsty said, staring down at the compass. "And I guess the clue means that we have to look underneath the toothbrush constellation!" She peered up at the sky and frowned. "But where is it?"

"It's vanished!" Rachel gasped. "Look, Jack Frost has got both his arms now. He must have stolen all the stars from the toothbrush constellation."

"Not quite," Zara chimed in. "I know the usual positions of the stars so well that I can see there's still one bit of the toothbrush left. Look at that lone star just there." And Zara pointed her wand at a single star twinkling away on its own. "That's what's left of the toothbrush constellation."

Just then the girls heard footsteps behind them, and Zara quickly whisked out of sight.

"Hi, you two," Kirsty called as a glum-looking Alex and Lucas came towards them. "How are you getting on?"

"Not very well," Lucas sighed. "We were trying to make our way to the first location underneath the slipper constellation, but so many of the stars have moved that now we're lost."

"You're heading in the right direction," Rachel told them, pointing towards the first signpost.

"Thanks!" Lucas and Alex looked more cheerful and dashed off.

"Let's hurry, Rachel," Kirsty said anxiously, "before all the toothbrush disappears!"

Fixing their eyes on the single star, the girls headed to the west of the campsite. As they went, they met several other children who were lost and confused because of the shifting stars, and Rachel and Kirsty helpfully directed them to the first location.

But as the girls went on their way, using their torches to light up the darkness, Kirsty suddenly tripped over something. She gasped, staggered and almost fell.

"Kirsty, are you OK?" cried Zara, flying off her shoulder.

"I'm fine," Kirsty replied. She shone her torch downwards and saw that the laces on one of her trainers had come undone. Kirsty bent to retie it, but then, to her surprise, she noticed tiny pinpricks of glitter on the ground. "Zara, Rachel, look at this!" she called.

Zara swooped down to see. "That's my star dust!" she exclaimed. "But how did it get there?"

Rachel moved her own torch slowly across the ground, picking out the specks of fairy dust. "I think they've been trodden into the ground by someone," she declared. "See those big, clumsy footprints?"

"Goblin footprints!" Kirsty gasped. "Those two rude little boys must be goblins in disguise! They're the only ones who are ahead of us."

"And they've got my bag of star dust!" Zara added.

Glow-in-the-dark Goblins!

"Well, at least they've left us a trail of star dust to follow to the second location!" Rachel said with a grin. In the torchlight, the three friends could see the star dust sparkling into the distance. "Off we go!"

The trail of glittering fairy dust led Zara and the girls through the campsite and towards the entrance to Camp Stargaze.

"I think the second location must be near the gate to the camp," Kirsty said.

"Look, it's right underneath the only star left of the toothbrush constellation."

"You're right, Kirsty," Rachel added, directing the beam of her torch at the camp entrance. "I can see a signpost with '2' on it. There's a big silver foil star pinned on the gate, too."

"And there are the glow-in-the-dark goblins!" Zara whispered.

The goblins, still covered in stickers, were kneeling on the ground under the signpost.

They were greedily scooping up handfuls of star-shaped chocolates and shoving them into their pockets.

"More prizes!" yelled the biggest goblin, who had glowing stars stuck on each ear like giant earrings.

"Stop that!" Kirsty called. "Those chocolates are for everyone!"

The smaller goblin, who had a star sticker on the end of his long, pointy green nose, scowled at her.

"Go and find your own prizes!" he shouted, grabbing the last few chocolates. Then both goblins jumped up and raced off into the dark Whispering Wood. Dazzling specks drifted around them, leaving a trail of fairy dust through the trees.

"I'll turn you into fairies, girls," Zara said. "Then we can chase after the goblins quickly, and without being seen." She fluttered above the girls' heads, showering them with fairy magic from her wand. Instantly Rachel and Kirsty shrank down to the same size as Zara with delicate, glittery wings on their backs.

"There go the goblins!" Zara called as they saw two glowing figures dart between the trees. "We can follow them easily, even in the dark, because of those star stickers they're wearing. Come on!"

44

Zara, Rachel and Kirsty zoomed into the Whispering Wood. For a moment they couldn't see the goblins at all, but then Kirsty spotted a faint glow through the undergrowth.

"There they are!" she whispered.

The goblins were running along one of the paths in the wood. Zara and the girls followed them at a safe distance, swerving neatly around the trees and keeping well out of sight. At last the goblins skidded to a halt beside a tall oak tree. Immediately Zara, Rachel and Kirsty landed on a branch just above their heads and hid among the leaves.

"I think we've got away from that pesky fairy and her silly friends at last!" the biggest goblin panted. "Let's eat our chocolate."

Zara and the girls watched as the goblins sat down under the tree and began to empty their pockets, heaping the chocolate stars on the grass. Then they saw the biggest goblin take out a shiny satin bag and throw it on top of the pile of chocolates.

"It's my bag of star dust!" Zara whispered.

The goblins unwrapped some of the chocolate and scoffed it greedily.

"Jack Frost is going to be very pleased with his constellation," the smallest goblin said smugly.

He opened Zara's bag and tossed a handful of magical dust onto the grass, where it sparkled like tiny jewels. "Maybe he'll give us another prize!"

The biggest goblin didn't answer because he was cramming another chocolate star into his mouth. Just then Zara and the girls saw one of the Blue Bunting birds flying towards them.

Rachel and Kirsty were amazed by how big the bird was now that they were fairy-sized. Looking rather forlorn, the Blue Bunting landed on the same branch where the three friends were perched.

"This poor bird must be lost," Zara whispered.

Suddenly the bird fluttered off the branch again and swooped down to the ground, skimming right over the top of the goblins' heads. They shrieked with fear.

"What's that?" the biggest goblin wailed through a mouthful of chocolate.

"It must be a pogwurzel!" the other goblin yelled, shivering and shaking all over. "Let's get out of this scary dark wood!"

Quickly the biggest goblin grabbed
the bag of star dust and the remaining
chocolates and then they both took to
their heels. Zara, Rachel and Kirsty flew
after them, but then
Rachel noticed the
light of a torch
ahead of
them.

"Someone's
coming!" she
whispered
to Zara and
Kirsty, and
the three of them
ducked behind a bush.

A moment later, Peter came down
the path and bumped right into the two
goblins.

"Aha, so you're the boys who've
stolen all the prizes!" Peter said crossly,
spotting the chocolates the biggest goblin
was carrying. Rachel, Kirsty and Zara
breathed a sigh of relief when they realised
that, although Peter had a torch, the
goblins' faces were hidden in the shadows.

"That's very greedy. Give them back, please." And he held out his hands.

"My bag of star dust is right in the middle of that pile of chocolates!" Zara said anxiously. "We can't let the goblins hand it over to Peter."

"Don't worry," Rachel replied, "I have an idea. Quick, Zara, make me and Kirsty human-size again!"

Scary Shadows

Immediately Zara swished her wand and Kirsty and Rachel shot back up to their normal size in a cloud of fairy dust.

"Hello, Peter," Rachel called, running out from behind the bush. Kirsty followed, wondering what Rachel's plan was. "We found those chocolates in the woods," Rachel went on, "and these boys are helping us to carry them back to the signpost by the gate."

"Yes, that's exactly what we're doing!" the smallest goblin chimed in quickly.

"Oh, so it wasn't you who took them," Peter said to the goblins. "Sorry about that. OK, make sure you put them back so that the others can find them." And with a smile, he went off. Kirsty and Rachel heaved sighs of relief.

"We just helped you, so now you can help us," Rachel told the goblins. "Give us the bag of star dust, please." She pointed up at the sky where the Jack Frost constellation now had legs. "It's time the

stars were back in their proper place."

"And you can go and put the chocolates back, too," Kirsty added.

The goblins glanced at each other. "You must be joking!" the smallest goblin yelled. He grabbed some of the chocolates from the other goblin and began throwing them at the girls. The biggest goblin joined in, pelting Rachel and Kirsty so hard with chocolates that they were forced to run back towards the bush to escape.

"Stop it!" Zara shouted, flying out from behind the bush to see what was going on.

Having used up all the chocolates, the goblins turned and dashed off. The biggest goblin was still clutching the bag of star dust tightly.

"After them, girls!" called Zara, waving her wand around Rachel and Kirsty.

When the girls were fairy-sized again, they all zoomed after the two goblins. They were running along one of the paths that led back to Camp Stargaze.

"We won't be able to chase the goblins through the camp," Rachel pointed out, dismayed. "Someone might see."

"Maybe we should keep them here in the Whispering Wood," Kirsty suggested. "They're nervous because it's dark and scary."

"You're right, Kirsty," Zara agreed. "It might be our best chance of getting my bag away from them. Let's chase the goblins back among the trees!"

The three friends linked hands and flew very fast so that they could get in front of the goblins. Then they swooped down, hovering in front of them and blocking their path.

"It's those fairies again!" the biggest goblin shouted, spinning around. "Quick, run the other way!" And the two goblins charged back into the thickest part of the wood.

"Quickly, girls!" Zara whispered.

Rachel, Kirsty and Zara whizzed around the goblins, herding them deeper into the wood. Whenever one of the goblins tried to take a path that led back to the campsite, Zara and the girls would zoom down and block their way.

"But how are we going to get the bag of star dust back?" Kirsty panted as she flew around the goblins' heads. "We need a plan!"

All of a sudden, though, Kirsty's heart began to pound with fright. A great black shadow was flying through the darkness, heading

straight towards her. Quickly she swerved
out of its way, but when it
came closer she was
very relieved to
see that it was
only one of the
Blue Bunting
birds fluttering
through the trees. It had looked very
dark and scary with its giant wings and
enormous beak.

"Oh!" Kirsty exclaimed, flying over to
Rachel and Zara. "I think I know how
we can get the bag of star dust back from
the goblins!" She took her fairy-sized torch
out of her pocket. "Look…"

Kirsty switched the torch on and pointed
the beam at Zara. Instantly a gigantic
shadow with enormous wings and long

arms and legs appeared on the broad
trunk of a tree behind her.

"Look!" the biggest goblin shouted,
pointing at the shadow looming over
them. "What's that?"

Rachel grinned. She flew into the
torchlight too, and a
second enormous
shadow sprang up
next to Zara's.

"There's
another!"
the small
goblin
yelped.

With a
quick flick
of her wand
Zara spun a

cloud of magical fairy dust around herself and the girls.

"WE'RE WATCHING YOU!" Zara called to the goblins. But her spell had changed her sweet, silvery voice to a loud, scary roar.

"YOU SHOULDN'T HAVE STOLEN ALL THE PRIZES!" said Rachel, trying not to laugh as her voice, now as loud and frightening as Zara's, boomed through the tree. "THAT WAS VERY NAUGHTY!"

"They must be pogwurzels!" the big
goblin wailed, terrified.

"And they're not just pogwurzels,"
moaned the small goblin. "They're giant
pogwurzels! Help!"

Rachel switched her torch on too,
and she, Kirsty and Zara took turns at
swooping around in front of the beams
of light, casting their huge shadows all
over the trees around them. The goblins
moaned with fear and clung to each other,
their knees knocking together.

"DROP THE BAG OF STAR DUST AND WE'LL LET YOU GO!" Kirsty roared in her pogwurzel voice.

Would the goblins give in and return Zara's bag?

Starry Party

The goblins stared at each other in a panic.

"What shall we do?" groaned the big goblin. "Jack Frost will be really angry if his constellation disappears!"

"Do you want to get eaten by pogwurzels instead?" the small goblin demanded. "Which is worse – Jack Frost or pogwurzels?"

The big goblin hesitated for a moment. Then he yelled "Pogwurzels!" Quickly he hurled the bag high in the air towards the giant shadows, and then he and his friend dashed off through the trees.

Smiling, Zara zoomed over and tapped the bag with her wand. It immediately shrank down to fairy-size and Zara caught it as it fell. "We did it, girls!" Zara declared happily. "Now everything in the night sky will soon be back to normal. Let's go and see."

Rachel and Kirsty followed Zara as she flew upwards through the trees.

Then they hovered above the
Whispering Wood, staring at the sky. The
stars were already sliding away from Jack
Frost's arms and legs and back to their
own constellations. As the girls watched,
Jack Frost gradually got smaller and
smaller until only his icy grin was left.
Soon, even that was gone.

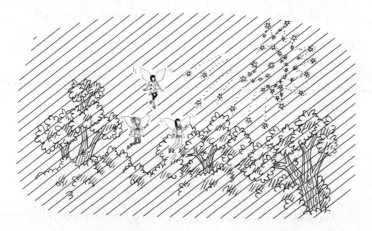

"All the stars are back in the right
place," Rachel sighed happily. "The night
sky looks beautiful."

"And the birds can find their way again," Kirsty added as the flock of Blue Buntings swooped past them calling happily to each other.

"I must give everyone in Fairyland the good news," Zara said as they floated down to land at the edge of the wood. She showered her magic fairy dust over the girls and they instantly shot up to their normal size again. "Thank you, girls. You're both stars! Keep up the good work!"

Rachel and Kirsty waved goodbye as Zara vanished in a mist of golden sparkles.

"Look, the pyjamas constellation is the only one on the map left to find now, and it's right above the observatory," Rachel pointed out as they went back to camp.

"And there's the third signpost outside the observatory door," said Kirsty. "This is the last location."

All the other children, including Alex and Lucas, were also heading to the observatory.

"Now that the stars are back in their proper places, they can follow their maps!" Kirsty whispered to Rachel as Peter gathered everyone round.

"Well done!" Peter said. "Can anyone put the three locations together and solve the puzzle?"

Everyone started talking, trying to work it out.

"The first location was in the camp among the tents," Kirsty murmured to Rachel.

"The second was the gate with the silver star on it," said Rachel.

"And the third was the observatory," Kirsty added. "And we gaze at the stars from the observatory, so it must be—"

"CAMP STARGAZE!" the girls called together.

"You've got it!" Peter said, and
everyone applauded. "Now, come into the
observatory. Professor Hetty and I have a
surprise for you."

Everyone crowded into the observatory
where Professor Hetty was waiting for
them. The walls were decorated with
glow-in-the-dark stars and there was a
table laid with sandwiches and cakes.

"It's a starry party!" Professor Hetty laughed, handing out glasses of squash. "It's been fun watching the strange events in the sky, but I'm glad everything's back to normal."

As the party got underway, Rachel and Kirsty sneaked a peek through the giant telescope.

"There's Zara!" Kirsty whispered, pointing to a golden light floating in the sky.

As the girls watched, the golden light burst into a shower of sparkles. Then the sparkles formed themselves into a dazzling constellation in the shape of a fairy. It hung there glittering in the sky for a few moments, and then disappeared.

Rachel and Kirsty glanced at each in delight. It was a wonderful ending to yet another thrilling fairy adventure!

RAINBOW magic

The Twilight Fairies

Now Rachel and Kirsty have helped
Zara, it's time to help...

Morgan the Midnight Fairy

The Midnight Hour

"I'm not tired at all, are you?" Kirsty Tate asked her best friend Rachel Walker. It was late at night and the two girls were in the Whispering Wood, shining their torches into the shadows as they collected firewood. They were staying with their families at a holiday centre called Camp Stargaze, and tonight the whole camp were having a midnight feast together.

"Not a bit," Rachel replied, tugging at a branch from the undergrowth. "I'm way too excited to even think about being tired!" She grinned at Kirsty. "What a brilliant holiday this is turning out to be.

A whole week together, lots of adventures, a midnight feast and…" She lowered her voice, glancing around cautiously."And plenty of fairy magic too!"

Kirsty smiled. It was true – she and Rachel had been having a wonderful time so far this week.

On their very first evening in camp, they'd met Ava the Sunset Fairy, who was one of seven Twilight Fairies. The Twilight Fairies looked after the world between dusk and dawn, making sure that everything was as it should be with the help of their special bags of magical dust. But a few nights ago, naughty Jack Frost had stolen these bags while the seven fairies were having a party together.

Kirsty and Rachel were friends with the fairies and had had lots of exciting adventures with them before, so when the Twilight Fairies asked if they would help search for the stolen fairy dust, Kirsty and Rachel were happy to say yes.

So far they had found three bags of magic dust belonging to Ava the Sunset Fairy, Lexi the Firefly Fairy and Zara the Starlight Fairy, but there were still four left to find.

It was a chilly night and Kirsty and Rachel were pleased to see that the moon and stars were shining brightly. "Zara's starlight magic is working perfectly again," Kirsty said, gazing up at the twinkling stars. She gathered some more sticks, humming cheerfully to herself.

It was going to be such fun tonight! A big fire was being lit, and then there would be lots of fireworks on the stroke of midnight, followed by a feast for everyone.

As the girls made their way through the dark wood, they heard a voice calling: "Kirsty, Rachel, is that you? We've found loads of firewood down here!"

"Follow our torchlights!" shouted a second voice, and then the girls saw bright white beams of light flashing through the trees in the distance...

Read the rest of

Morgan
the Midnight Fairy

to find out what magic happens next...

Available now!

Florence the
Friendship Fairy

Out now!

978-1-40831-238-4
£5.99

Can Kirsty and Rachel find the three lost
magical items that Florence needs to keep
friendship special?

Have you checked out the

website at:

www.rainbowmagicbooks.co.uk

Meet the Showtime Fairies

out now!

Madison the Magic Show Fairy
978-1-40831-286-5

Leah the Theatre Fairy
978-1-40831-287-2

Alesha the Acrobat Fairy
978-1-40831-288-9

Darcey the Dance Diva Fairy
978-1-40831-289-6

Amelia the Singing Fairy
978-1-40831-291-9

Isla the Ice Star Fairy
978-1-40831-292-6

Taylor the Talent Show Fairy
978-1-40831-290-2

The Twilight Fairies

For Grace Massie,
with lots of love

Special thanks
to Sue Mongredien

ORCHARD BOOKS
338 Euston Road, London NW1 3BH
Orchard Books Australia
Level 17/207 Kent Street, Sydney, NSW 2000
A Paperback Original

First published in 2010 by Orchard Books

HiT entertainment

Illustrations © Orchard Books 2010

A CIP catalogue record for this book is available
from the British Library.

ISBN 978 1 40830 907 0

1 3 5 7 9 10 8 6 4 2

Printed in China by Imago

The paper and board used in this paperback are natural recyclable
products made from wood grown in sustainable forests. The
manufacturing processes conform to the environmental regulations
of the country of origin.

Orchard Books is a division of Hachette Children's Books,
an Hachette UK company

www.hachette.co.uk

Lexi
the Firefly
Fairy

by Daisy Meadows

ORCHARD BOOKS

www.rainbowmagic.co.uk

The
Fairyland
Palace

Observatory

Games
Area

Fairy Homes

Ferry

CAMP
STAR GAZE

Mirror Lake

The Twinkling Tree

Starry Glade

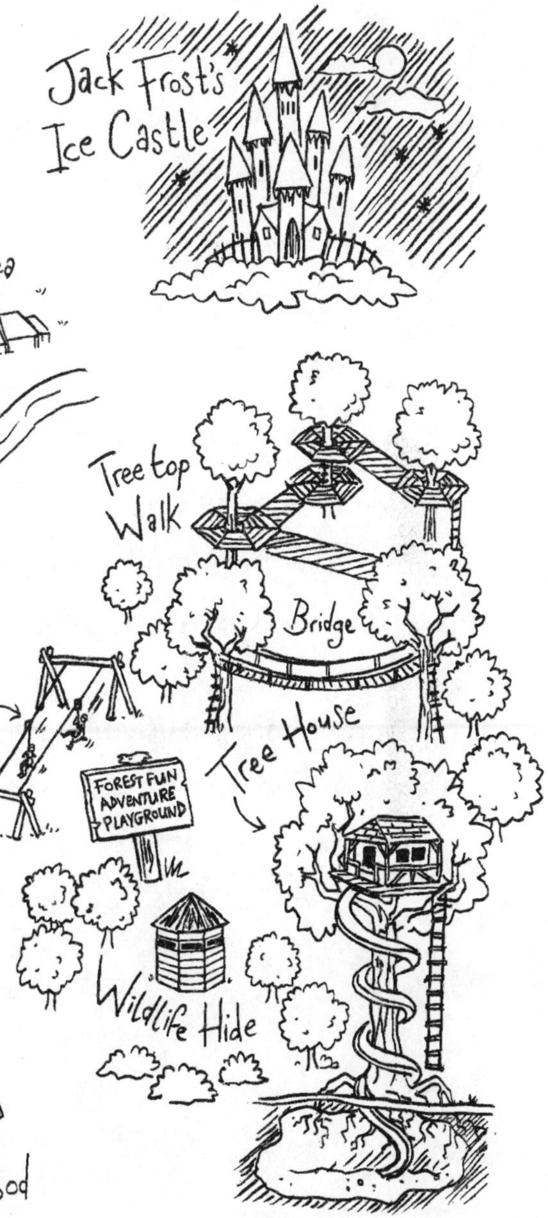

Jack Frost's
Ice Castle

Tree top
Walk

Bridge

Tree House

FOREST FUN
ADVENTURE
PLAYGROUND

Wildlife Hide

The Twilight Fairies' magical powers
Bring harmony to the night-time hours.
But now their magic belongs to me,
And I'll cause chaos, you shall see!

Sunset, moonlight and starlight too,
There'll be no more sweet dreams for you,
From evening dusk to morning light
I am the master of the night!

Contents

A Face in the Bushes

The sun was just setting and the evening starting to grow chilly at Camp Stargaze. Rachel Walker zipped up her fleece and tucked an arm through Kirsty Tate's to keep warm. Rachel and Kirsty were best friends, and their families had come on a camping holiday together for a week.

Exciting things always seemed to happen when the two girls got together – and so far, this holiday was already looking like it would be another very magical one!

Kirsty and Rachel were gathered with about twenty other children at the edge of the campsite. There was going to be a special night-time walk, and everyone was chattering excitedly as they waited to set off.

"Is everyone ready? Then let's go into the Whispering Wood!" called Peter, one of the play-leaders. Kirsty and Rachel walked with the rest of the group into the woodland.

It was cool and dark underneath the leafy trees, and Kirsty flicked on her torch and shone it around. The tall trees swayed in a gentle breeze, and their leaves really did seem to make a whispering sound. "It's creepy being here in the evening, isn't it?" she said to Rachel.

"I know," Rachel replied, glancing into the undergrowth. "Makes you wonder what's in those shadowy corners."

"Whoooo-oooo-oooo!"

Rachel and Kirsty clutched at each other as they heard a ghostly wailing behind them. They spun

11

round to see two boys, Lucas and Matt, laughing so hard they were bent double. "Gotcha!" Matt chortled.

"Your faces! You looked terrified!" Lucas added, his eyes sparkling with mischief.

Kirsty and Rachel laughed too, once their hearts had stopped racing. Those boys! Then Rachel had an idea, and winked at Kirsty. "Oh my goodness!" she said, pretending to gasp in fright. "Look up there – two glowing eyes staring down at us!"

The boys gazed at the tree where Rachel was pointing – and now it was their turn to look scared. "No way!" Matt yelped in alarm. Shining out of the darkness were two gleaming lights, which looked exactly like the eyes of a wild animal. "What is it, do you reckon? A panther?"

"Hmmm," said Kirsty, pretending to think. "It looks like it's a really dangerous…*firefly* or two!" She and Rachel giggled. The glittering lights in the tree were only a couple of flickering fireflies – there was nothing scary or dangerous about them!

Peter, the leader, had overheard. "Wait until we get to the Twinkling Tree," he said. "It always has masses of fireflies around it. It's pretty high up, so the lights of the fireflies can be seen from far away, drawing other fireflies towards it." He grinned. "When they're all twinkling on the branches it's like a Christmas decoration. Or even a magical fairy tree!"

Rachel and Kirsty smiled at one another. They knew all about fairy magic! They were friends with the fairies, and often helped them – especially if horrid Jack Frost and his sneaky goblin servants had been up to their usual tricks!

The group started climbing a hill but Matt stopped walking suddenly. "What was that? I just heard something," he said, shining his torch into the dark undergrowth.

Kirsty rolled her eyes at Rachel. "Not trying to scare us again, are you, Matt?" she said.

Matt shook his head. "No – honestly! I heard a rustling sound in the bushes. Listen!"

The girls stopped and listened. Matt was right – there was a rustling noise nearby. "Do you get bears out here?" Lucas wondered nervously.

15

Peter smiled and shook his head. "No," he said. "It's probably just a badger. Nothing to worry about."

Rachel, Kirsty, Lucas and Matt all shone their torches into the bushes. Rachel hoped it was a badger – she'd never seen one before.

"There – a face!" Lucas cried out, pointing. He gulped. "I saw a face...but it was green. What could that be?"

Matt started joking about aliens, but Peter said calmly that it was probably just animals moving the green leaves around, which had only looked like a face. Rachel and Kirsty exchanged a worried look, though. They were pretty sure the green face didn't belong to an alien or an animal, but was something much worse: one of Jack Frost's naughty goblins!

The Twinkling Tree

"Are you thinking what I'm thinking?"
Rachel asked Kirsty in a low voice.

Kirsty nodded. "Goblins!" she whispered.
"There were goblins about yesterday,
when we helped Ava the Sunset Fairy,
weren't there? There might be more
tonight."

The day before, the girls had met the seven Twilight Fairies, who looked after the world between sunset and sunrise — but all was not well. The Twilight Fairies had been having a Twilight Party under the stars when mean Jack Frost and his goblins had stolen their magic bags of twilight dust from under their pillows! Since they'd been without their magic dust, strange things had been happening at night, such as the bright green sunset which had appeared the night they'd arrived at Camp Stargaze.

"I wonder if we're going to have another fairy adventure tonight," Rachel whispered, her arms prickling with goosebumps. "I hope so!"

"Me too," Kirsty said eagerly. "Let's keep a look-out for anything magical."

The group of campers continued slowly up the hill. "I can't see any fireflies now," Rachel realised, gazing at the dark branches of the trees. "I wonder if they're all in the Twinkling Tree?"

"Probably," Kirsty said. "I can't wait to see it."

After a few more minutes, Peter stopped and spoke to the group. "We should get our first glimpse of the Twinkling Tree soon," he said. He started walking again, still talking. "Once we climb up the last steep bit of the hill, you'll see it shining through the trees. Any minute… Now! Oh." Disappointment filled his voice.

"That's strange," he said. "Where are they?"

Rachel and Kirsty had reached the top of the hill too. They could see a tall, majestic tree through the dusky sky, but its long, leafy branches were empty, without a single firefly to be seen.

Peter frowned. "That's a shame," he

said. "Usually the Twinkling Tree is a real highlight of this walk. Where can all the fireflies be?"

Kirsty felt disappointed but then Rachel nudged her. "Look," she hissed. "What's that?"

A small spark of light was dancing through the air towards them, and Kirsty  peered through the darkness to make out its shape. Was it a firefly…or could it be a fairy? Somebody else had noticed the moving light too.

"Hey – look!" called Matt excitedly. "There's a firefly. Quick, steer it towards the Twinkling Tree so it can signal to its friends!"

The firefly – if it was a firefly – swerved away abruptly as Lucas and Matt ran towards it. Rachel and Kirsty peered into the darkness, but the light vanished before they could see for sure what it was.

Then Lucas gave a yell. "There's more of them over here!" he shouted, pointing at a cluster of sparkling lights that whizzed and danced through the air in the distance.

The other children rushed to see the sparkles and Kirsty was about to run after them, but Rachel put a hand on her arm. She had just noticed a tiny gleaming figure slip out of the shadows and fly towards them.

"Look!" she hissed excitedly as she recognised the fairy's pretty, smiling face, blonde wavy hair held back in a green band, and a twinkling silver sequinned miniskirt, with baseball boots to match. It was Lexi the Firefly Fairy!

"Hello again," Kirsty said in delight, holding her jacket pocket wide open so that Lexi could dive into it and hide.

"Phew!" said Lexi. "That was close – I thought those boys had spotted me. I had to conjure up some flying sparkles in the nick of time!"

Kirsty and Rachel moved out of sight, behind the low-hanging branches of the Twilight Tree. "Good thinking," Rachel grinned.

"It's nice to see you again, Lexi. We were wondering what had happened to the fireflies that usually gather here. Do you know?"

"I do," Lexi said. "It's all because of Jack Frost. He knows how important the fireflies are. Not only do they make summer nights special in the human world with their lovely flickering lights, but they also provide light to the Fairyland Palace, and the fairies' toadstool houses, too. Usually, I have my magic bag of fire dust which keeps the fireflies lit up. But since Jack Frost and his goblins stole my dust, the fireflies' lights have gone out – and Fairyland is in darkness!"

"Oh no," Kirsty said. "Can we help look for your bag of fire dust? We helped Ava find her sunbeam dust yesterday."

"I heard," Lexi said. "That's really good news! And yes please, I'd love you to help me too. Would you mind coming to Fairyland with me?"

"Mind?" Rachel echoed. "We'd love to!" She and Kirsty knew that they were quite safe to leave the other children as time always stood still while they were in Fairyland. They would be able to fly off and have an exciting adventure, and nobody in the human world would notice they'd gone!

"Fantastic," Lexi replied. "First, let me turn you into fairies…" She waved her wand over the two girls and they felt their bodies shrink smaller and smaller, until they were the same size as Lexi. Both girls had glittering fairy wings on their backs and they fluttered them in delight.

"Now let's go to Fairyland!" Lexi cried, throwing more fairy dust over the three of them.

A sparkling whirlwind spun around, and Kirsty and Rachel were whirled up into the air. Another fairy adventure was beginning!

Fairyland in Darkness

After several moments, Rachel and Kirsty felt themselves gently landing again. The glittering whirlwind cleared...and both girls blinked in surprise. Usually when they came to Fairyland, it was light and sunny there, with sweet little toadstool houses and flowers everywhere, and the beautiful Fairyland Palace gleaming on the hillside.

Tonight, however, most of Fairyland was pitch black, and it took a moment for the girls' and Lexi's eyes to adjust to the darkness.

"Wow," Rachel said, peering into the gloom. "Where are we? I can hardly see a thing!"

The end of Lexi's wand was sparkling and she held it up in front of them like a torch. They could just see the vague outline of a toadstool house in front of them, with its sloping roof and little wooden door. "I think this is where Summer the Holiday Fairy lives," Lexi replied –

and at that moment, the door of the house opened, and out came Summer herself.

"Lexi, is that you?" she asked, shivering. "Flicker's light won't go on."

"Where are you, Flicker?" Lexi called. "Are you there?"

From out of the darkness came the sound of beating wings, and then an insect flew over and landed on Lexi's palm. Neither Rachel nor Kirsty had ever seen a firefly close up before, and they gazed in interest at Flicker's sleek black and gold shell.

He was about the size that a robin would be to them in the human world, and his expression was sad.

"I usually sit on Summer's windowsill in the evenings to give her light," Flicker explained. "Then, once she's gone to bed, I fly to the stream with my friend Glimmer. There's a night rose that grows there, and the nectar is delicious." His antennae drooped miserably. "But without my light, Glimmer won't be able to find me. And neither of us will be able to find the rose!"

"Oh dear," Lexi said, stroking Flicker's back. "I'm sorry to hear that. We're

searching for my magic bag of fire dust
and as soon as we find it, I'll be able
to turn all the
fireflies' lights on
again, but until
then—"

Lexi stopped
talking, her face
alert. Kirsty
and Rachel
became aware
of a commotion nearby, and listened.
They could hear voices – loud, and
argumentative, coming nearer by the
second.

"You've got it all wrong!" the first voice
grumbled. "I've caught four, and you've
caught two. It's no good pretending you
got the last one, because you didn't."

"I totally did! You're making things up!" the second one shouted. "You're just jealous because I'm better at catching them than you!"

Kirsty and Rachel shrank into the shadows as the voices came nearer still. They would know those bad-tempered, harsh-sounding voices anywhere – they belonged to the goblins!

"What are they up to, I wonder?" Summer whispered, as they stood huddled in her doorway.

They didn't have to wait long to find out. The goblins suddenly came into view, and the four friends saw that they were carrying torches, which cast golden beams through the darkness. They also held what looked like lanterns, but there was no light coming from them.

When the goblins spotted the fairies gathered outside Summer's house with Flicker on Lexi's palm, they looked delighted. "Aha! There's another!" the tallest goblin shouted and then, before the fairies could stop him, he snatched Flicker, shoved him into a lantern…and ran off!

"Hey!" shouted Lexi, but it was too late. The goblins had vanished into the distance. The four fairies could now see other shadowy figures running around, all with lanterns. From the goblins' shouts of glee, it was clear that they were stealing every firefly they could find.

"What are they doing? Why are they taking the fireflies?" Rachel asked, bewildered.

"I don't know," Lexi said grimly, "but I bet it's got something to do with Jack Frost, and my fire dust! I'm going to follow them, and see what's happening."

"We'll come with you," Kirsty offered at once.

"And I'll warn the other fairies what the goblins are up to," Summer vowed.

"Thanks, Summer," said Lexi, then she turned to Kirsty and Rachel. "Come on — there's no time to lose!

Follow Those Goblins!

Kirsty, Rachel and Lexi set off through the darkness. It was easy to follow the goblins, because they were so noisy, and also because they had their torches, which lit the way. The three friends hung back in the shadows so as not to be spotted.

After a few minutes on the goblins' trail, Lexi's eyes narrowed. "They're going to Jack Frost's Ice Castle," she whispered.

"What *is* he plotting, I wonder?"

As they rounded a corner, the three fairies gasped in disbelief. Jack Frost's castle was usually a grim, forbidding place with its icy walls and patrolling guards, but this evening, it looked positively cheery and welcoming, lit up as it was against the dark sky. "Wow!" Kirsty breathed. "I've never seen it so beautiful."

"Yes," Lexi said, sounding cross. "And it's only beautiful because he's used my special fire dust to light up all the fireflies he's got trapped in lanterns, look!"

As Rachel and Kirsty flew across the moat, closer to the castle, they realised that Lexi was right. Glowing lanterns hung in every window, and inside each lantern flickered a firefly. "How selfish!" Rachel fumed. "Stealing all the fireflies and trapping them, just so that his castle can be lit up!"

"I know," Lexi said. "The poor things. They aren't as bright as they usually are – they must be feeling very sad."

"Look, there's Jack Frost," Kirsty hissed, seeing the spiky, cold figure appearing in his doorway. "Hide!"

The three fairies hid inside a bush, and Lexi muttered some magic words which made the light of her wand go out. They peered through the leaves to see Jack Frost holding a small bag which cast a magical glow into the murky waters of his moat. As the goblins trooped into the castle with their lanterns full of fireflies, Jack Frost sprinkled fire dust on each firefly, making them light up. "Now it won't be dark any more," Jack Frost said gleefully, a smug smile on his face.

"They've caught so many," Rachel said. "I bet it was a goblin Lucas saw in the Whispering Wood. Jack Frost must have sent the goblins into the human world to steal fireflies there, as well as Fairyland!"

"We've got to rescue the fireflies," Lexi said. "We can't leave them trapped in lanterns, as Jack Frost's prisoners. They should be free to fly around wherever they please!"

Kirsty and Rachel agreed. But how could they release the fireflies when they were right under Jack Frost's nose?

"We'd be able to sneak into the castle if it was dark," Kirsty said, "but we can't chance it now, with the fireflies' lights flashing on and off. We'd be seen straightaway."

Rachel thought. "Is there a way to tell the fireflies to turn their lights off?" she wondered. "That would make everything dark again."

Lexi nodded. "I could use my wand to show them," she replied, sounding more cheerful. "Let's see if this works."

She fluttered above the bushes and muttered some magic words which made the tip of her wand sparkle and shine through the dark sky.

Then, with another magical command, she turned the wand's light off.

Lexi, Kirsty and Rachel held their breath as they stared at the fireflies. Had they seen Lexi's light? Had they understood the message?

Some of the fireflies' lights vanished, making the castle slightly darker, but most of the lanterns remained lit up.

"I'll try again," Lexi said, turning the light of her wand on again, and then off. This time, more of the fireflies seemed to have seen her light, and understood the message. Lots of their little lights turned to black and the castle became much darker.

"It's working," Kirsty said excitedly. "Clever fireflies!"

Lexi turned her wand on, then off one more time, and the last remaining fireflies turned their lights off too – plunging Jack Frost's castle into total darkness.

"What's going on? Turn those lights back on!" the girls heard Jack Frost splutter. Then they heard his footsteps hurrying into the castle, and heard him shouting frantically to his servants.

"Now's our chance, come on!" Lexi hissed, and she, Kirsty and Rachel tiptoed towards the castle. Rachel hardly dared breathe as they crept silently up to the doorway.

Would Jack Frost see them? And what would he do to them if he did?

Glow, Glow, Glow!

Rachel, Kirsty and Lexi pressed close to the walls as they sneaked through the open doors of Jack Frost's Ice Castle. They could hear his booming voice from further within the castle ordering the lights to be put on, but managed to escape down one of the corridors without anyone noticing them.

The three friends flew silently along the corridor, their eyes straining to see through the darkness. They fluttered into every room they could find, opening the lanterns and setting the fireflies free.

"Quick, back to the fairy houses, you'll be safer there," Lexi whispered to the fireflies.

It was tricky, trying to work quickly in the darkness – and nerve-racking too, when they could hear Jack Frost bellowing in the background. "What's wrong with this fire dust? Why have the fireflies stopped shining? I don't want it to be dark!" he yelled.

"Hurry, hurry," Lexi urged Kirsty and Rachel. "We've got to be as fast as we can!"

As the fireflies flew out of the castle windows, they turned on their flickering lights once more. It was lovely to see them whizz through the darkness like tiny shooting stars, twinkling in the night sky, one after another.

On and on the fairies flew, from room to room, releasing the fireflies. The goblins had obviously told Jack Frost that the fireflies were escaping because the three friends heard him shout with rage, ordering his goblins to chase after the fireflies and catch them again. "I will not put up with this darkness!" he thundered.

"He's so silly!" Lexi sighed. "The fireflies are so friendly they would happily light up his castle if he just asked them. Why did he have to try to trap them? They'll stay well away from him now."

"At least they can still glow from the magic dust Jack Frost sprinkled on them," Rachel pointed out, opening another lantern and setting free the firefly inside it. "They can fly back to the toadstool houses now – and hopefully the Twinkling Tree too."

"Yes," Lexi agreed, "but the fire dust on them won't last forever, unfortunately." She opened another lantern to let out the firefly, and watched as it flew away. They were right at the very top of Jack Frost's castle now, and the firefly soared into the air, its light gleaming. "There," she said. "That's the last one. The fireflies are all free!" She put her hands on her hips. "Now we just need to get my bag of fire dust off Jack Frost and we can get out of here."

Kirsty swallowed nervously. "How are we going to do that?" she wondered aloud. Sneaking into the

Ice Castle and setting the fireflies free had been scary enough, but the thought of trying to get Lexi's bag of fire dust from Jack Frost was even scarier!

There was silence while they all thought. It was hard to concentrate, though, when they could still hear Jack Frost shouting at his goblins. "I need those fireflies back NOW!" he bawled.

His words gave Rachel an idea. "Jack Frost really wants the fireflies… so maybe we could somehow trick him into thinking *we're* fireflies," she suggested.

"Yes! If you could use your magic, Lexi,

to make us look like fireflies, it'll mean
we can get close to him — close enough to
grab the bag of fire dust!" Kirsty added.

"That's a great idea," Lexi said,
waving her wand in
a complicated
pattern. Streams
of bright magic
spiralled from the
end of it, swirling
all around.

Seconds later,
Kirsty and Rachel
felt themselves
shrinking smaller and
smaller, until Lexi seemed like a giant
next to them. "Now to make you glow,
glow, glow!" Lexi smiled, waving her
wand again.

Rachel giggled as she felt a fizzing sensation all over – and looked down at herself to see that her legs and feet were shining brightly. "Cool!" she laughed.

The three of them flew out of the window, Kirsty and Rachel gleaming in the darkness just like two little fireflies. They swooped low over the goblins who were gathered outside with Jack Frost. Jack Frost saw them and gave a shout. "There are two more! Catch them!"

Rachel and Kirsty zipped

away in different directions with goblins chasing after each of them. Rachel flew in loop-the-loops, while Kirsty flew in a zigzag pattern, making the goblins puff and pant to keep up.

Rachel was getting rather dizzy with all her looping, and decided to zoom straight ahead, the goblins still chasing her. But Kirsty had had the same idea, and was also whizzing along in a straight line – and she was headed straight for Rachel!

"Watch out!" Lexi called in alarm. "You're going to crash!"

Firefly Magic

At the very last moment, Rachel swerved
out of the way of Kirsty, and Kirsty
managed to zip up high in the air. But
the goblins who'd been chasing after them
weren't quite so nimble – and ended up
crashing into each other, and knocking
over Jack Frost!

Just then, the moon slid out from behind
a cloud, casting a silvery light over the
grounds of the castle. Rachel saw to
her excitement that Jack Frost had three
or four goblins piled on top of him and
couldn't move. Even better, she
could see Lexi's bag of fire
dust sticking out of his
pocket!

She darted
down, her heart
thumping, and
just managed
to pull out
the bag of
dust and fly
into the air
with it.

It was

rather heavy, but luckily, Lexi had seen her, and quickly waved her wand to make the bag light enough for Rachel to carry.

Then Lexi soared over to Rachel, and took the bag gratefully from her. "Well done!" she exclaimed. "Come on, let's get out of here before they untangle themselves!"

The three friends flew over the moat and landed briefly so that Lexi could turn Kirsty and Rachel back into fairies.

They were just about to set off again, when Lexi noticed a group of fireflies, including Flicker, on a thorny bush. Strange! Why hadn't they flown off with the others?

"Are you all right?" she asked the fireflies.

"We're fine," Flicker replied, wiggling her antennae happily. "In fact, we're more than fine. We've found a lovely patch

of night rose plants here with plenty of delicious nectar, so we're going to make a new home here together."

"Oh, OK," Lexi replied. She smiled at Kirsty and Rachel. "At least Jack Frost and the goblins will have some light now, I suppose."

Once they were back in the Fairyland village, Lexi gathered all the fireflies that had come from the human world and waved her wand, sending them back to the Whispering Wood, together with Kirsty and Rachel.

As the sparkly whirlwind vanished, Kirsty and Rachel found themselves still fairy-sized, and right at the top of the Twinkling Tree, along with hundreds of flickering fireflies!

"Wow!" cried the children below, gazing up at the tree which was now twinkling and sparkling all over, thanks to the fireflies' lights.

"They're back!" Peter shouted in delight. "There – doesn't it look amazing?"

Up in the tree, Lexi hugged Kirsty and Rachel goodbye. "Thanks for everything," she said. "Now I'd better turn you back into your usual size, so you can see how pretty the tree looks from the ground too!"

With a last wave of Lexi's wand, Kirsty and Rachel felt their bodies tingle with fairy magic... and seconds later, found themselves at the back of the group, gazing up at the Twinkling Tree.

"Oh, wow," Rachel sighed. "It's beautiful!"

"The fireflies look like fairies," said a little girl nearby, and Rachel and Kirsty turned to grin at one another.

70

If only the girl knew that they had been fairies up there in the tree just seconds earlier!

"That was really exciting," Kirsty said happily. "Definitely the most de-light-ful adventure yet!"

RAINBOW magic

The Twilight Fairies

Now Rachel and Kirsty have helped
Lexi, it's time to help...

Zara the Starlight Fairy

A Star is Born!

"This telescope is huge, Kirsty!" Rachel Walker said excitedly to her best friend, Kirsty Tate. "I can't wait to have a look at the night sky."

"It's going to be amazing," Kirsty agreed as they stared up at the enormous silver telescope.

The girls were spending a week of the summer holidays with their parents at Camp Stargaze, which had its very own observatory for studying the stars. The observatory was a square white building topped with a large dome, and charts and pictures of the night sky hung on the walls.

In the middle of the observatory stood the gigantic telescope, and Professor Hetty, the camp astronomer, was explaining to Rachel, Kirsty and the other children about the stars and constellations.

"As you know, this area was chosen for Camp Stargaze because we can get really clear views of the night sky from here," Professor Hetty reminded them. She was a jolly, round-faced woman with twinkling blue eyes and a mop of red hair.

"Have any of you ever done a join-the-dots puzzle?"

All the children looked puzzled, but everyone nodded.

"Well, a constellation is rather like a join-the-dots puzzle!" Professor Hetty explained with a smile. "A constellation is made of individual stars that join up to make a picture, just like the puzzle. But although the stars look close together to us here on earth, sometimes they're actually millions of miles apart! Let's take a look, shall we?"

Professor Hetty pressed a button on the wall. There was a noise overhead, and Rachel and Kirsty glanced up to see a large section of the domed roof slide smoothly back, revealing the dark, velvety night sky and the sparkling silver stars twinkling here and there like diamonds in a jewellery box. Everyone gasped and applauded.

"Wonderful!" Professor Hetty said eagerly. "I never get tired of looking at the night sky. It's so magical."

Rachel nudged Kirsty. "Professor Hetty doesn't know just how magical the night-time really is!" she whispered.

Kirsty smiled. When she and Rachel had arrived at Camp Stargaze, Ava the Sunset Fairy had rushed from Fairyland to ask for their help. The girls had discovered that Ava and the other six Twilight Fairies made sure the hours from dusk to dawn were peaceful and well-ordered, with the help of their satin bags of magical fairy dust.

But while the Twilight Fairies were enjoying a party under the stars with their fairy friends, Jack Frost had broken into the Fairyland Palace with his naughty goblin servants. The goblins had stolen the magical bags that were hidden under the Twilight Fairies' pillows. Then, with a wave of his ice wand, Jack Frost had sent the goblins and the bags spinning away to

hide in the human world. Jack Frost's plan
was to cause night-time chaos for both
fairies and humans, but Rachel, Kirsty
and the Twilight Fairies were determined
not to let that happen.

"I wonder if we'll meet another Twilight
Fairy today?" Kirsty murmured to Rachel
as they all lined up to have a look through
the telescope. "I'm so glad we managed to
find Ava's and Lexi's magical bags, but we
still have five more to go!"

"Remember, we have to let the magic
come to us," Rachel reminded her.

The girls' new friend, Alex, was first
to use the telescope, and Professor Hetty
showed her how to look through the
eyepiece. Alex peered into the telescope
eagerly.

"Everything looks so close!" she gasped.

"Can you see any pictures in the stars, Alex?" asked Professor Hetty.

"I think I see something…" Alex peered more closely. "Oh!" She burst out laughing. "I can see a constellation shaped like a toothbrush!"

"Well done," said Professor Hetty. "And those of you who aren't using the telescope should be able to see it too, if you look hard…"

Read the rest of

Zara
the Starlight Fairy

to find out what magic happens next...

Available now!

Florence the Friendship Fairy

Out now!

978-1-40831-238-4
£5.99

Can Kirsty and Rachel find the three lost
magical items that Florence needs to keep
friendship special?

Have you checked out the

website at:

www.rainbowmagicbooks.co.uk

Meet the Showtime Fairies

out now!

Madison the Magic Show Fairy
978-1-40831-286-5

Leah the Theatre Fairy
978-1-40831-287-2

Alesha the Acrobat Fairy
978-1-40831-288-9

Darcey the Dance Diva Fairy
978-1-40831-289-6

Amelia the Singing Fairy
978-1-40831-291-9

Isla the Ice Star Fairy
978-1-40831-292-6

Taylor the Talent Show Fairy
978-1-40831-290-2

The Jewel Fairies

For Danni who loves fairies

Special thanks to
Narinder Dhami

ORCHARD BOOKS
338 Euston Road, London NW1 3BH
Orchard Books Australia
Hachette Children's Books
Level 17/207 Kent Street, Sydney, NSW 2000
A Paperback Original
First published in Great Britain in 2005
Rainbow Magic is a registered trademark of Working Partners Limited.
Series created by Working Partners Limited, London W6 OQT
Text © Working Partners Limited 2005
Illustrations © Georgie Ripper 2005
The right of Georgie Ripper to be identified as the illustrator
of this work has been asserted by her in accordance
with the Copyright, Designs and Patents Act, 1988.
A CIP catalogue record for this book is available
from the British Library.
ISBN 1 84362 958 5
1 3 5 7 9 10 8 6 4 2
Printed in China

India
the Moonstone
Fairy

by Daisy Meadows

illustrated by Georgie Ripper

ORCHARD BOOKS

www.rainbowmagic.co.uk

By Frosty magic I cast away
These seven jewels with their fiery rays,
So their magic powers will not be felt
And my icy castle shall not melt.

The fairies may search high and low
To find the gems and take them home.
But I will send my goblin guards
To make the fairies' mission hard.

Contents

A Nasty Nightmare

"Kirsty, help!" Rachel Walker shouted.
"The goblins are going to get me!"

Panting, Rachel glanced behind her.
She was running as fast as she could,
but the green goblins were getting closer
and closer. They were grinning nastily,
showing their pointed teeth. Now one
of them had grabbed Rachel by the

shoulder, and was shaking her hard—

"Rachel?" Kirsty Tate was leaning over her friend's bed, shaking her awake. "Wake up! You're having a nightmare."

Rachel woke and sat up in bed. "What time is it?" she asked. "I dreamt that there were horrible goblins chasing me, and I couldn't escape."

"It's 7.30," Kirsty replied, perching on the edge of the bed. "Why were the goblins after you?"

Rachel frowned. "I can't remember," she sighed. "But you know what, Kirsty? I've got a funny feeling that Jack Frost might be up to something again!"

Kirsty's eyes opened wide. "Oh, do you really think so?" she gasped. "Then maybe our fairy friends will need our help!"

Rachel and Kirsty shared a magical secret. They had become friends with the fairies, and whenever there was a problem in Fairyland, Kirsty and Rachel were called on to help.

The fairies' greatest enemy was Jack
Frost. He was always looking for ways to
make trouble, helped by his mean goblin
servants. Not long ago, Jack Frost had
tried to ruin the celebration party for
King Oberon and Queen Titania's 1000th
jubilee. But luckily, Kirsty and Rachel
had come to the rescue.

"We'll have to keep our eyes open,"
Rachel agreed. "If the fairies need our
help, they'll let us know somehow."

Kirsty nodded. "Well, it's only the
beginning of half-term, and I'm staying
with you for the whole week," she pointed
out. "So we have plenty of time."

Before Rachel could reply, the sweet,
tinkling sound of music suddenly filled
the room. Both Kirsty and Rachel jumped.

"What's that?" Kirsty asked.

Rachel looked puzzled for a moment, but then she began to laugh. "It's my music box!" she smiled, pointing at the dressing-table. "The one the Party Fairies gave us."

After helping the Party Fairies to
stop Jack Frost from spoiling the
jubilee celebrations, Rachel and Kirsty
had each been given a beautiful,
musical jewellery box with a tiny
fairy on top. Rachel's box sat on her
dressing-table, and the girls could see
that the fairy was spinning round in
time to the music.

"Yes, but how did
it start up on its
own?" Kirsty
asked, with a
frown. "I didn't
wind it, and
you've only just
woken up."

"Look!" Rachel
gasped. "The box is glowing!"

Rachel scrambled out of bed, and she
and Kirsty rushed over to take a closer
look. Rachel was right. The box was
glowing with a faint pink light which
shone from under the closed lid.

"Lift the lid, Rachel," Kirsty
whispered.

Hardly daring to breathe, Rachel
reached out and slowly lifted the lid.

Immediately a glittering shower of
multi-coloured fairy dust burst from the
jewellery box. It swirled around the
girls, wrapping them in a cloud of
sparkles and lifting them off their feet.

Fairy News

After just a moment or two, the sparkles began to drift away and the girls felt their feet lightly touch the ground. Rachel and Kirsty blinked a few times and looked around.

"Kirsty, we're in Fairyland!" Rachel gasped.

"In our pyjamas!" Kirsty added.

17

The girls were now fairy-sized with glittering fairy wings on their backs, and they were standing in the golden Great Hall of the fairy palace. King Oberon, Queen Titania and a small crowd of fairies stood in front of them. The girls noticed that they all looked worried.

Queen Titania stepped forwards. "You are very welcome, girls," she said with a smile. "I hope you don't mind us bringing you here so unexpectedly."

"Of course not," Rachel said quickly.

"You have been such good friends to us in the past," the Queen went on, "that we were hoping we could call on you again, now that we are in trouble."

"What's wrong?" asked Kirsty anxiously.

"Let me explain," the Queen replied sadly. "Every year, at Halloween, we have a huge celebration in Fairyland. All the fairies have to recharge their fairy magic for another year."

"So every fairy in Fairyland parades around the Grand Square," King Oberon put in. "Then they all march into the palace to a very special chamber, where Queen Titania's tiara rests upon a velvet cushion."

"It sounds wonderful," Rachel sighed, hoping that she and Kirsty might be allowed to watch the grand procession one day.

Queen Titania nodded. "It is," she replied. "And my tiara is very important for fairy magic. It has seven beautiful jewels set in it. A sparkling fountain of fairy dust pours from each of the seven jewels, and they join together to form one great, glittering rainbow of magical fairy dust."

Kirsty and Rachel were listening carefully, their eyes wide.

"What happens then?" Kirsty asked.

"Each fairy must dip her wand in the rainbow fountain to recharge it," the Queen explained. "Then she will be able to perform magic for another year."

The King shook his head sadly. "But now Jack Frost has put a stop to all that," he sighed. "Two nights ago, he crept into the palace and stole the seven jewels from the Queen's tiara!"

"Oh, no!" Rachel and Kirsty exclaimed together.

"Our special celebration was to take place in a week's time," the Queen went on, looking worried. "So the fairies' magic is already running low."

"The jewels must be returned to the tiara," King Oberon added, "before the fairies run out of the jewels' magic completely!"

"Does this mean that there will be no magic at all left in Fairyland?" asked Kirsty anxiously.

"Not exactly," the Queen replied. "Fairy magic isn't quite as simple as that. Some magic, like Weather Magic and Rainbow Magic, aren't controlled by by the jewels."

"But the jewels do control some of the most important kinds of fairy magic," the King explained. "Like flying, wishes and sweet dreams. Some people have already started to have nightmares."

Rachel nodded, thinking of her own scary dream. "We have to get the jewels back!" she said firmly.

"Where is Jack Frost now?" Kirsty wanted to know. "Has he taken the jewels to his ice castle?"

The Queen shook her head. "Jack Frost doesn't have the jewels any more," she said. "Come with me, and I will show you what happened."

Rachel and Kirsty followed the
fairies outside into the beautiful
palace gardens. They
stopped beside the
golden pool, its
surface as clear and
smooth as glass.

"Look," Queen
Titania said
softly, waving
her wand over
the water.

Immediately
tiny ripples began
to spread across the
surface of the pool.
The ripples grew bigger and
bigger, and slowly a picture
appeared on the water's surface.

"It's Jack Frost!" Rachel exclaimed. Tall, thin, spiky Jack Frost stood in front of Queen Titania's golden tiara upon its velvet cushion. The seven magic jewels glittered as dazzling streams of magic dust poured from each one. Laughing, Jack Frost thrust his snowflake-tipped wand into the magic rainbow fountain, where it glowed like fire. "He is recharging his magic," the King explained.

Kirsty and Rachel watched in dismay as Jack Frost then prised the sparkling gems from the golden tiara. He waved his wand and immediately the jewels were encased in solid ice.

"What is he doing?" Rachel asked, puzzled.

"The light and heat of the jewels' magic makes them difficult for cold, icy creatures like Jack Frost and his goblins to hold," Queen Titania explained. "Look."

Now Jack Frost was whizzing back to his ice castle, carried by a frosty wind which blew him along. He carried the jewels in his arms, but Rachel and Kirsty could see that the hard shell of frost around them was already beginning to melt.

Jack Frost swooped down from the grey sky and landed in the throne room of his ice castle. By this time the frost around the jewels had almost melted away. The jewels glowed, casting shimmering rays of light like laser beams into every corner of the icy room. Goblins came running to see the gems, wearing sunglasses to protect their eyes from the glare.

"Stand back, you fools!" Jack Frost roared, waving his wand again and

casting another spell to cover the jewels with ice. But the jewels were still glowing, and the ice began to melt away almost immediately.

"Look, master," yelled one of the goblins suddenly, "the fairy magic is melting your castle!"

Jack Frost looked round in a fury. Sure enough, water was beginning to trickle down the icy walls, and there was a puddle at the foot of his throne.

"Jack Frost's magic is not strong enough to block the power of the jewels," Queen Titania told Rachel and Kirsty.

The girls watched as the goblins began rushing around, mopping up the water as fast as they could. But as quickly as they cleared one puddle away, two more appeared.

"Very well then," shouted Jack Frost, stamping his feet in rage. "If I cannot keep these magic jewels, no one else shall have them! I will cast a spell to get rid of them." And he raised his wand high above his head.

Lost!

"Oh, no!" Kirsty gasped. She and
Rachel watched in horror as an icy
blast of wind whipped up around the
throne room. The glowing jewels
were sent spinning and tumbling
across the room and out of the
window, where they scattered far
and wide.

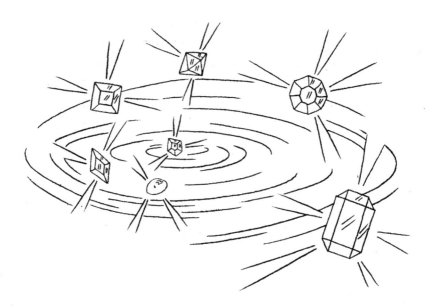

"See how the jewels grow larger as they fall into the human world?" Queen Titania pointed out, just as the picture in the pool began to flicker and fade. "Because they are magical, they'll hide themselves until we can find them and bring them back to Fairyland."

The picture in the pool was fading fast. But just before it disappeared,

Rachel saw one of the jewels, a creamy-coloured stone, fall into someone's back garden. With a start of surprise, Rachel realised that she knew exactly whose garden it was!

The Queen was shaking her head sadly as the picture vanished completely. "All of our fairy seeing magic is used up," she sighed. "So the pool can't show us where all the jewels have gone."

"But I know where one of them is!" Rachel burst out excitedly. "I recognised the garden where it fell!"

Everyone turned to stare at her.

"Are you sure, Rachel?" Kirsty asked.

Rachel nodded. "It was Mr and Mrs Palmer's back garden," she explained. "The Palmers are friends of my parents, and I've been to their house loads of times to help Mum babysit their little girl, Ellie."

One of the fairies was so excited at this that she whirled up into the air, her long brown hair streaming out behind her. "I'm India, the Moonstone Fairy," she cried, her eyes shining. "And I'm sure it was my Moonstone which fell into your friends' back garden!"

The little fairy wore a pretty dress with a nipped-in waist and floaty skirt.

The dress was white, but every time India moved, flashes of shimmering pink and blue shot through the material. On her feet she wore dainty white sandals.

"You must meet all our Jewel Fairies," said King Oberon, as the other fairies crowded around. "Each one is responsible for teaching all the other fairies how to use her jewel's magic." He pointed at India the Moonstone Fairy. "India teaches dream magic, while Emily the Emerald Fairy teaches seeing magic, Scarlett the Garnet Fairy teaches growing and shrinking magic, Chloe the Topaz Fairy teaches changing magic, Sophie the Sapphire Fairy teaches wishing magic, Amy the Amethyst Fairy teaches appearing and disappearing magic, and Lucy the Diamond Fairy teaches flying magic."

Rachel and Kirsty smiled round at all the fairies.

"We'll do our best to get your jewels back," Kirsty said.

"Thank you," the fairies replied.

"We knew you would help us," Queen Titania said gratefully. "But Jack Frost knows we will be trying to find the jewels, and he has sent his goblins into the human world to guard them."

"The goblins will find it difficult to pick the jewels up," King Oberon went on. "The bright light and magic of the gems will burn them, because they belong to the cold, icy world of Jack Frost. Instead, the goblins will probably lurk near the jewels and try to stop us getting them back."

Rachel and Kirsty nodded thoughtfully.

Queen Titania looked grave. "So now we need your help not only to find each magic jewel," she finished, "but also to outwit the goblins that will be guarding them!"

On the Right Track

"We'll find a way to get the jewels back," Rachel said firmly, and Kirsty nodded.

King Oberon smiled at them. "And you will have our Jewel Fairies to help you."

Rachel frowned. "I had a dream about the goblins chasing me," she said slowly.

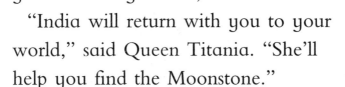

India sighed, looking very sad. "Without the Moonstone, the fairies' power to send sweet dreams into the human world is fading," she explained. "That's why you had a nightmare, Rachel."

"India will return with you to your world," said Queen Titania. "She'll help you find the Moonstone."

"We know we have to look in the Palmers' back garden," Kirsty said. "But how will we know where to search for the other jewels?"

Queen Titania smiled. "Just as before, you must let the magic come to you," she replied. "The jewels will find you.

And remember, they have grown bigger
in the human world, so they will be
easier to spot."

Rachel and Kirsty nodded. Then India
fluttered over to join them and the
Fairy Queen raised her wand.

"Good luck!" called the fairies, as the
Queen waved her wand and Rachel,
Kirsty and India disappeared in a
shower of magic sparkles.

When the cloud of fairy dust vanished,
Rachel and Kirsty realised that they
were back in Rachel's bedroom.

"We must get to work right away,
girls!" called a silvery voice.

The girls turned and saw India
perched on the dressing-table mirror.

"Yes, let's go over to the Palmers' house now," said Rachel eagerly, making for the door.

Kirsty burst out laughing. "I think we'd better change out of our pyjamas first, don't you?"

"Good idea!" Rachel grinned.

"How can we get into the Palmers' back garden?" India asked, as the girls quickly got dressed.

"We could throw a ball over the fence," Kirsty suggested. "Then we could ask the Palmers if we can pop into their garden to find it."

"Yes, that would work," Rachel agreed.

"Girls, are you awake?" Mrs Walker's voice drifted up the stairs. "Breakfast's ready."

India fluttered across the room and hid

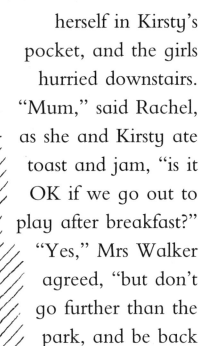

herself in Kirsty's pocket, and the girls hurried downstairs. "Mum," said Rachel, as she and Kirsty ate toast and jam, "is it OK if we go out to play after breakfast?" "Yes," Mrs Walker agreed, "but don't go further than the park, and be back in time for lunch."

"Thanks, Mum." Rachel said, slipping out of her chair.

Kirsty did the same. "We need a ball," she whispered as they went to get their jackets.

"There's one in the shed, I think," Rachel replied.

The girls found a tennis ball and then set off down the road. Although it was autumn, it was quite a warm day and the sun shone down brightly from a blue sky.

"I hope my Moonstone is safe," India said softly, popping her head out of Kirsty's pocket. "I wonder if there are any goblins guarding it."

"We'll soon find out," Rachel replied, stopping in front of a house with a bright red door. "This is the Palmers' house."

The house was only three doors away from Rachel's home, on the corner of the street. Rachel took the ball out of her pocket, slipped round the corner and tossed it over the fence into the back garden. Then she joined Kirsty and India again in front of the house.

"I'll knock on the door," Rachel said, leading the way up the path.

"Let's hope they're in!" replied Kirsty.

Rachel rang the bell, and they waited for quite a while. Just as the girls and India were starting to give up hope, the door opened.

"Hello, Rachel," beamed Mrs Palmer. "And you must be Kirsty. Rachel told me she was having a friend to stay."

"Hello," Kirsty said politely.

"Sorry to disturb you, Mrs Palmer," Rachel said, "but I'm afraid we just lost our ball over your fence."

Mrs Palmer smiled. "As a matter of fact, I was just sitting in the back garden with Ellie. I didn't see your ball come over, though. Do you want to come and look for it?"

"Yes, please," Rachel replied.

"If you don't mind," added Kirsty.

Mrs Palmer opened the door wide. "Go straight through, girls. I'm just 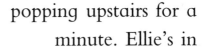 popping upstairs for a minute. Ellie's in her pram on the patio, if you want to say hello."

Rachel led Kirsty through the kitchen and out through the back door.

India popped her head out of Kirsty's pocket. "The Moonstone's here somewhere," she cried happily. "I can feel it!"

"It's a big garden," Kirsty said. "We better start looking right away." She and India hurried over to the nearest flowerbed and began to peer among the shrubs. Meanwhile, Rachel went across the patio to say hello to Ellie. But as she walked towards the pram with its pretty white sunshade, Rachel began to shiver.

Suddenly there was a chill in the air.
A loud wail came from the pram.

Ellie had started to cry.
Ellie must be feeling
the cold, too, Rachel
thought. But it was
quite warm until
a moment ago!
Mrs Palmer rushed
out of the house and
ran over to the pram. "It's very
strange, Rachel," she said, as she
pushed back the sunshade and bent
down to pick up the baby. "Ellie's
always had trouble sleeping, but ever
since we got this mobile for her pram
yesterday, she's been sleeping ever so
well." Mrs Palmer frowned, lifting
Ellie out from under her lacy blanket.

"Something seems to be upsetting her today though; she's been very restless."

As Mrs Palmer picked Ellie up, the baby stretched out her chubby little hand to grab one of the decorations hanging from the mobile. Rachel looked at it more closely. It was hung with silver stars, yellow suns and pale moons. And then, suddenly, her heart missed a beat, for there, glittering in the middle of the mobile, was a cream-coloured stone which flashed with pink and blue light.

The Moonstone! Rachel thought excitedly. *No wonder Ellie's been sleeping well. She must have been having extra-sweet dreams!*

"I'm just going to take Ellie inside," said Mrs Palmer. "There's a chill in the air, all of a sudden."

"I hope that doesn't mean that some of Jack Frost's goblins are nearby," Rachel murmured to herself.

Leaving Mrs Palmer wrapping Ellie in a blanket, Rachel ran down the garden towards Kirsty and India, who were searching round the birdbath in the middle of the lawn.

"I've found the Moonstone!" Rachel whispered triumphantly. "It's hanging in the middle of the mobile on Ellie's pram."

"Wonderful!" India gasped.

"Well done, Rachel!" added Kirsty.

"Mrs Palmer's taking Ellie inside," said Rachel. "We can get the Moonstone as soon as she's gone."

The girls and India watched as Mrs Palmer carried Ellie into the house. Then Rachel and Kirsty immediately ran towards the pram, with India flying along beside them. But before they reached it, the door of the garden shed flew open with a crash, and two green goblins rushed out!

Hot Pursuit!

"The Moonstone is ours!" one of the goblins yelled. "And we'll never let the fairies have it back!"

"Never! Never!" shouted the other goblin.

As Kirsty, Rachel and India watched in horror, he leapt up onto the pram and grabbed at the string on which the

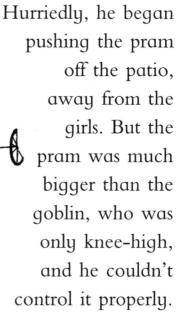

Moonstone was dangling.

"He's going to take the Moonstone!" Rachel gasped. "Stop him!"

As the girls rushed towards the pram, the other goblin panicked. Hurriedly, he began pushing the pram off the patio, away from the girls. But the pram was much bigger than the goblin, who was only knee-high, and he couldn't control it properly.

It bumped and bounced over the grass and onto the garden path. The goblin inside was caught off-balance.

With a screech of rage, he tumbled over and got caught up in the baby's blankets, before he could grab the Moonstone.

Kirsty, Rachel and India chased after the pram as the goblin charged down the garden path, pushing it in front of him. They could see the Moonstone swinging wildly on the mobile, but they couldn't reach it — the goblins were too far ahead. The pram bounced and jolted its way along, while the goblin inside was struggling to free himself from the tangle of blankets, and he shouted crossly at his friend to stop.

Then, all of a sudden, one wheel hit
a large stone lying in the middle of the
path. The pram was going so fast that
it overturned. Both goblins let out shrill
cries of alarm as they flew through the
air. And then they both landed in a
heap, covered in Ellie's sheets and
blankets, underneath a large fir tree.

"India, can you stop the goblins from getting away?" Kirsty panted, as she and Rachel chased down the path towards the goblins.

"I have a little dream magic left which might send the goblins to sleep," India replied. She zoomed ahead of the girls and hovered over the goblins, waving her wand. A few sparkles of fairy dust drifted down onto the goblins, who stopped struggling to free themselves and began yawning and rubbing their eyes instead.

"I'm so tired!" one of them sighed.

"And this blanket is really warm and cosy," the other one said sleepily. "I think I might have a little nap."

"Me too," the first goblin agreed. "Sing me a lullaby."

"No, you sing a lullaby!" the second goblin demanded.

"No, YOU!" yelled the first.

"They're waking themselves up with their silly argument!" Rachel exclaimed. "What are we going to do?"

"I think I have an idea!" Kirsty whispered, hurrying towards the goblins.

Rock-a-bye
Goblins

Rachel and India watched as Kirsty began to tuck the goblins snugly into the blanket.

"Now, now, settle down," she said in a soft, sweet voice. "It's time for your nap."

The goblins stopped arguing and started yawning again.

"I am sleepy," the first goblin murmured, snuggling down under the pink blanket.

But the second goblin was trying hard to keep his eyes open. "Wasn't there something we were supposed to be doing?" he asked.

Rachel hurried over to help Kirsty. "Go to sleep now," she said in a soothing voice. "You can worry about that later."

And Kirsty began to sing a lullaby to the tune of *Rock-a-bye Baby:*

"Rock-a-bye Goblins wrapped in a rug,
Asleep in the garden, all nice and snug,
When you wake up from your little nap,
You will find India's got her stone back."

By the second line of Kirsty's little song, both goblins were snoring soundly.

"Well done, Kirsty," Rachel said with a grin. "But we can't leave the goblins here for Mrs Palmer to find!"

"Leave that to me," India replied. She waved her wand over a large branch of the fir tree. Immediately, the branch drooped lower, so that the leaves completely covered the sleeping goblins.

"Perfect!" Kirsty declared. "The goblins are green like the leaves, so they'll be well hidden until they wake up."

India and Rachel laughed.

"Then they'll have to rush back to Jack Frost and tell him they've lost the Moonstone," India said. "They'll be in big trouble!"

Chuckling quietly, the girls picked up the pram and pushed it back to the patio. Then, as India watched in delight, Kirsty carefully took the magic Moonstone from the middle of the mobile. It flashed and gleamed in the sunlight.

"We mustn't spoil Ellie's mobile," India said. She waved her wand and a glittering, shiny bubble appeared in place of the Moonstone on the mobile.

As it caught the light, it sent rainbow-colours shining in all directions.

"And now," India went on, "the Moonstone is going straight back to Fairyland and the Queen's tiara, where it belongs!" She touched her wand to the jewel. Immediately a fountain of sparkling fairy dust shot up into the air and the Moonstone vanished.

"Thank you, girls," India said,
giving Rachel and
Kirsty a hug.
"I must go home
now, but I hope
you'll be able to
help the other Jewel
Fairies find their
magic stones too."

"We'll do our best!"
Rachel promised.

"Goodbye, India!"
Kirsty added, as
their fairy friend
flew away in a
cloud of sparkles.

"I wonder where
the other six jewels are
hiding," Rachel murmured.

"And I wonder if we'll have to face many more goblins," Kirsty said with a frown.

Rachel shivered, remembering her nightmare. "I just hope I don't dream about them again tonight," she said.

Kirsty laughed. "Don't worry, Rachel," she told her friend. "India's got the Moonstone back now; she's sure to send you sweet dreams!"

The Jewel Fairies

India has got her moonstone back.
Now Rachel and Kirsty
must help

Scarlett the Garnet Fairy

Win a Rainbow Magic
Sparkly T-Shirt and Goody Bag!

In every book in the Rainbow Magic Jewel Fairies
series (books 22-28) there is a hidden picture of a jewel with
a secret letter in it. Find all seven letters and
re-arrange them to make a special Fairyland word,
then send it to us. Each month we will put the entries into a
draw and select one winner to receive a
Rainbow Magic Sparkly T-shirt and Goody Bag!

Send your entry on a postcard to Rainbow Magic Jewel
Competition, Orchard Books, 96 Leonard Street,
London EC2A 4XD. Australian readers should
write to Hachette Children's Books, Level 17/207
Kent Street, Sydney, NSW 2000.
Don't forget to include your name and address.
Only one entry per child. Final draw: 30th September 2006.

Coming Soon...

Stella the Star Fairy

STELLA THE STAR FAIRY

1-84362-869-4

Stella the Star Fairy can't keep Christmas
bright and shiny without her three magical
tree decorations. Can Kirsty and Rachel
help her get them back to the fairy tree
by Christmas Eve, or will the season
be ruined for everyone?

RAINBOW magic ®

by Daisy Meadows

All priced at £3.99. *Holly the Christmas Fairy*, *Summer the Holiday Fairy* and *Stella the Star Fairy* are priced at £4.99.
Rainbow Magic books are available from all good bookshops, or can be ordered direct from the publisher: Orchard Books, PO BOX 29, Douglas IM99 1BQ
Credit card orders please telephone 01624 836000
or fax 01624 837033 or visit our Internet site: www.wattspub.co.uk
or e-mail: bookshop@enterprise.net for details.

To order please quote title, author and ISBN and your full name and address.
Cheques and postal orders should be made payable to 'Bookpost plc.'
Postage and packing is FREE within the UK
(overseas customers should add £2.00 per book).
Prices and availability are subject to change.

Have you checked out the

Website at:

www.rainbowmagic.co.uk

There are games, activities and fun things to do, as well as news and information about Rainbow Magic and all of the fairies.

The Party Fairies

Cherry, Melodie and Grace have got
their magic party bags back. Now
Rachel and Kirsty must help

Honey the Sweet Fairy

Win a Rainbow Magic
Sparkly T-Shirt and Goody Bag!

In every book in the Rainbow Magic Party Fairies
series (books 15-21) there is a hidden picture of a magic
party bag with a secret letter in it. Find all seven letters
and re-arrange them to make a special Fairyland
word, then send it to us. Each month we will put the
entries into a draw and select one winner to receive a
Rainbow Magic Sparkly T-shirt and Goody Bag!

Send your entry on a postcard to Rainbow Magic
Competition, Orchard Books, 96 Leonard Street,
London EC2A 4XD. Australian readers should write
to 32/45-51 Huntley Street, Alexandria, NSW 2015.
Don't forget to include your name and address.
Only one entry per child. Final draw: 28th April 2006.

Coming Soon...
The Jewel Fairies

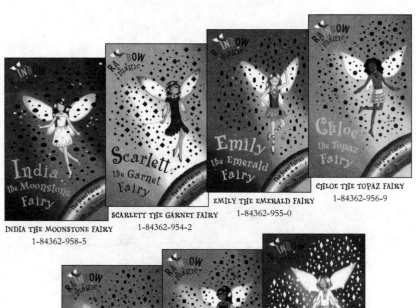

INDIA THE MOONSTONE FAIRY
1-84362-958-5

SCARLETT THE GARNET FAIRY   1-84362-954-2

EMILY THE EMERALD FAIRY   1-84362-955-0

CHLOE THE TOPAZ FAIRY
1-84362-956-9

AMY THE AMETHYST FAIRY
1-84362-957-7

SOPHIE THE SAPPHIRE FAIRY   1-84362-953-4

LUCY THE DIAMOND FAIRY
1-84362-959-3

Also coming soon . . .

SUMMER THE HOLIDAY FAIRY

1-84362-638-1

Summer the Holiday Fairy is getting all hot and
bothered, trying to keep Rainspell Island the best
place to go on vacation. Jack Frost has stolen the
sand from the beaches, and three magical shells.
The fairies need Rachel and Kirsty's help
to get the holiday magic back...

Have you checked out the

Website at:

www.rainbowmagic.co.uk

There are games, activities and
fun things to do, as well as news
and information about Rainbow
Magic and all of the fairies.

by Daisy Meadows

Ruby the Red Fairy	ISBN	1 84362 016 2
Amber the Orange Fairy	ISBN	1 84362 017 0
Saffron the Yellow Fairy	ISBN	1 84362 018 9
Fern the Green Fairy	ISBN	1 84362 019 7
Sky the Blue Fairy	ISBN	1 84362 020 0
Izzy the Indigo Fairy	ISBN	1 84362 021 9
Heather the Violet Fairy	ISBN	1 84362 022 7

The Weather Fairies

Crystal the Snow Fairy	ISBN	1 84362 633 0
Abigail the Breeze Fairy	ISBN	1 84362 634 9
Pearl the Cloud Fairy	ISBN	1 84362 635 7
Goldie the Sunshine Fairy	ISBN	1 84362 641 1
Evie the Mist Fairy	ISBN	1 84362 636 5
Storm the Lightning Fairy	ISBN	1 84362 637 3
Hayley the Rain Fairy	ISBN	1 84362 638 1

The Party Fairies

Cherry the Cake Fairy	ISBN	1 84362 818 X
Melodie the Music Fairy	ISBN	1 84362 819 8
Grace the Glitter Fairy	ISBN	1 84362 820 1
Honey the Sweet Fairy	ISBN	1 84362 821 X
Polly the Party Fun Fairy	ISBN	1 84362 822 8
Phoebe the Fashion Fairy	ISBN	1 84362 823 6
Jasmine the Present Fairy	ISBN	1 84362 824 4
Holly the Christmas Fairy	ISBN	1 84362 661 6